LAST
STOP

LAST STOP

THE DIAMOND KNIFE
BOOK ONE

DJANGO WEXLER

Podium

Copyright © 2024 by Django Wexler

Cover design by Jeff Brown

ISBN: 978-1-0394-7319-5

Published in 2024 by Podium Publishing
www.podiumaudio.com

Podium

For Little Z

LAST
STOP

CHAPTER
ONE

Well?" the bartender said, her husky whisper barely audible over the tavern buzz. "Are you staying the night?"

Zham Sa-Yool, political exile and aero pilot extraordinaire, took stock.

That the girl was attractive went without saying; dark curly hair, beautiful brown skin, and lips the color of a fresh bruise. She leaned forward over the bar to reach his ear, which caused her blue bartender's vest to fall open to a point somewhere just short of scandal. Her bare arms gripped the bar, well-muscled and banded with intricate black tattoos.

However.

Staying the night would cost money, and the current contents of Zham's purse (a couple of Markan half-crowns and assorted small change from half a dozen Imperial cities) would not be enough to cover the tab he'd already run up, much less any further adventures. The prudent thing to do would be to make his excuses and scuttle away.

"When you put it like that," he said, smiling broadly, "how can I say no?"

And then—because when the engine is on fire, why worry about chipping the paint?—he raised his voice and added, "And let me buy another round!"

The bartender straightened up, face dimpling in a matching smile, and rang the bell behind the bar. There was a wild cheer from all corners and flying foam from tankards raised in enthusiastic salute.

It was that kind of bar. Zham was something of a connoisseur of taverns, alehouses, watering holes, and other praxes of bibulation, and he tended to classify them according to vibes rather than trappings. The Zham General Theory of Bars started with the following question: if you took a fiddle and started sawing out a jolly tune, would the patrons a) begin dancing on the tables, or b) feed you your teeth? The former type were more pleasant, but the latter tended to be cheaper.

The Lonely Bug—the sign featured an amorous mantid—was decidedly a category a) sort of place, squeezed in between a cloth-traders' yard and a row of furniture workshops a few tiers up from the Low Docks. The ground floor had the bar and a few tables, while a rickety staircase led to a loft with an overhanging balcony. A few nooks in the balcony's shadow were blocked by curtains for those who wanted a semblance of privacy.

Tonight, the place was packed, a steady press of porters, drivers, furniture-makers, clothier's apprentices, butcher's boys, accounting clerks, extract refiners, and all the other types that made up the working class of a midsize Imperial city. Zham raised his mug—nearly empty; he'd have to do something about that—to acknowledge the cheer, then turned back to the bar. The bartender, whose name he muzzily recalled was Isabella, took his dregs and supplied a fresh helping.

"Don't forget we have plans," she said, raising one perfectly sculpted eyebrow. "I get off in half an hour."

"For certain," Zham said, with a return waggle of his somewhat-bushier brows.

He was feeling a few moments behind events and didn't quite understand the reminder until he noticed the jolly old gentleman on the seat to his right had been replaced by someone smaller and considerably more female. She was alternating between staring around at the bar and looking up at him. In either configuration her eyes were very wide, as though Zham and the Lonely Bug were tied at the top of her list of greatest things she'd ever seen.

She was, Zham decided, a note out of place. Seated, she was a head shorter than him, and her feet didn't come close to touching the ground. She wore a long duster designed for someone much broader in the shoulders, which hung off her like a cloak. Her skin was milk-pale, with a dusting of freckles across the bridge of her pug nose like a barista's artfully scattered chocolate powder, and her bright copper hair was a short, spiky mess. Isabella had set a mug of pale yellow beer in front of her, but she was so absorbed in looking around that she had yet to address it.

She was quiet for a few moments longer, and Zham was beginning to wonder if it was incumbent on him to start the conversation the girl was clearly intent on. Just then, she seemed to reach a decision and gave him a wide, guileless smile.

"You're Zham Sa-Yool, right? Of the *Last Stop*?"

Zham took a long pull from his beer to cover his initial reaction, which was to punch her in the face and run for it. There were any number of reasons someone could be looking for him, and most would be hazardous to his health. He didn't recognize the girl, but that didn't mean much. Some of the people he owed money to had quite a lot of friends.

In the end he refrained, more from sozzled sentiment than anything else. Punching her wide-eyed excitement would be like dropkicking a puppy.

"Mmm," he said, noncommittally.

"Only, I'm supposed to find Zham Sa-Yool," she said. "We were supposed to meet at the agent's office, but I waited for a couple of hours and he didn't show up. Eventually, she showed me a picture and said I could probably find him here."

"Oh." Zham stared into his half-empty mug as though it held answers. Memory was hard; it was always hard by this time of night, but he *thought* he recalled Quedra telling him something to that effect. Meet the new hire, bring her back to the ship, that sort of thing. He felt a wash of guilt, but it was brief and easily dispelled by another pull of beer.

He became aware that she was still staring at him. Zham cleared his throat, and—as so often happened—a brilliant idea occurred to him.

"You're late," he said.

"Late?" She blinked.

"Late. But"—he belched grandly—"you passed the test in the end. Congratulations."

"Test?" Her eyes somehow widened even further. "You mean—"

"Of course." He gave her a superior smile. "You want to fly for the *Last Stop*, I need to know you're up to the challenge!" He peered at her a little closer. "You do want to fly for the *Last Stop*, don't you?"

"I do!" she squeaked.

Gods only know why, Zham thought, but kept it to himself.

"Well," he said aloud, "being an aero pilot isn't just about flying, you know. You have to be able to handle yourself in any situation. Throw a punch, cheat at cards, find someone in the back of a bar in an Imperial armpit."

"I *see*," she said. He had the distinct impression that somewhere behind her eyes, she was taking furious notes.

"Right." Zham leaned on the bar and hoisted his glass, getting into his role. "So, what's your name?"

"Niko Fanucci," she said. "It's Nicolosa, really, but everyone calls me Niko."

"Very well, Niko-really-Nicolosa. How old are you?"

"Twenty." She looked defensive for a moment, as though she didn't expect him to believe it.

"And you can fly?"

She gave an eager nod. "Geoff Vanta sent me a recommendation."

Zham considered that. Vanta was a crusty old pirate, and if he said someone could fly that meant something. On the other hand, as far as Zham knew Vanta couldn't read, so his signature on a letter probably didn't. But it must have been good enough for Quedra, which meant Zham didn't really get a vote.

"Well," he said again. Wet brain cells sizzled slightly. "Right."

"Should we go to the ship?" she said.

He blinked at her. "What, now? It's only"—he glanced at his wrist, remembered he'd sold his watch a week before, and looked at the window instead—"not even dawn."

"If you were just waiting here for me, I mean," Niko said. "For the test."

Zham leaned forward and growled. "*Who said the test was over?*"

"You did!" Niko squeaked. "Um. Just now. You said I passed."

"Oh." He sat back. "Well, Niko, the night is young. Youngish. And I have plans." He wondered briefly if she would be amenable to joining the part of those plans that involved him and Isabella, but dismissed the thought as beneath him. He was still Navy enough that the idea of sleeping with someone under his command was like imagining sex with his sister. And *that* simile made his flesh crawl. "We'll need to find something for you, too. Drink your beer."

Niko looked down at the mug, which seemed very large in her small hands. "I don't really *like*—"

"*Niko!*" Zham roared.

"Yes?!"

"Proper carousing is *also* part of a pilot's job! If you might have to die for someone, you ought to get properly wrecked with them beforehand!"

"I'm not sure that I *exactly* follow—"

"And it's not just the drinking!" Zham was on a roll. "You like boys or girls?"

"Um." Niko sank downward into her mug until she was practically blowing bubbles in it, cheeks flaming red. "Girls. I think. But I haven't— I mean, I'm—"

She was saved from further embarrassment by a commotion near the Lonely Bug's front entrance. Given the level of noise in the bar, it was hard for any altercation to break through, but Zham had a very well-tuned ear for certain kinds of sounds and was able to detect voices raised in anger and the dull *thump* of somebody getting laid out. He turned away from Niko and craned his neck for a look, but all that was visible were a half dozen black fedoras poking up from the crowd.

Possible, of course, that this was the Fedora Enthusiasts' local meet-up. But it seemed unlikely. Zham boosted himself up onto the bar and slid down behind it, then grabbed the still-sputtering Niko and lifted her over bodily, coat flapping.

"What are you *doing*?" Isabella said. "Zham—"

Grabbing both women by the arm, Zham pulled them into a crouch.

"Quiet!" he hissed.

"*Zham*—" Isabella said.

"Zham—" Niko began.

"*Zham Sa-Yool*!" a deep voice bellowed from the front of the bar. "Where is he?"

Zham crab-walked along the length of the bar, pulling the pair of them behind him. At the far end, a curtain hung from the loft balcony, concealing a small niche that stored extra barrels of beer. He pressed into it with them and drew in a tight breath.

"What are we doing?" Niko whispered.

"Hiding," Zham whispered back.

"Why in here?"

"Because they'll look behind the bar."

"Why am *I* here?" Isabella said.

Zham frowned. It had seemed like the right move at the time. "To . . . keep you safe?"

"Safe from *who*—"

"Come on," the booming voice interrupted. "Zham Sa-Yool. We know he's here somewhere."

Zham could hear murmurs, but no one seemed to be shouting out "He's over there!" which was heartening. "This," he murmured to Niko, "is why you always stand your round."

"Zham, is this your wallet?" Isabella said.

"What?" He squirmed, but in the tight confines of the nook, he couldn't reach her. "What are you doing?"

"Under the circumstances, I thought I should take this chance to settle your tab," she said. There was a moment of silence after she got the wallet open. "Is this really all the money you have?"

Another pause. The deep-voiced stranger cursed and shoved his way closer.

"I was going to make *sure* my sister sent a draft . . ." Zham ventured.

Isabella was already pushing out through the curtain. "Hey! He's over here!"

The rumble of footsteps grew closer. Niko looked at Zham expectantly. He heaved a sigh.

"Stay here," he said. "When I shout your name, grab that curtain and yank on it as hard as you can. Really put your whole weight into it, understand?"

She gave an eager nod. Zham straightened his collar and stepped back into the light.

The vibe in the Lonely Bug had changed, and not for the better.

The crowd had emptied out some, and those who remained were pressed against the walls, leaving a big clear space in front of the bar.

Other patrons crowded the balcony, leaning over the rail to watch the excitement. Isabella had retreated to the other end of the bar, arms folded in a "none of this is my problem" sort of stance.

The main attraction, however, were the half dozen fedoras in the center of the room, or more precisely the walking slabs of beef in badly tailored dark suits underneath them. For a certain kind of professional, a suit is a necessity to look respectable, but an *expensive* suit was a waste, given the inevitably high wear-and-tear and dry cleaning bills.

While none of them were shrimps, they were led by an absolute mountain of a man, so tall Zham expected to see snow capping his peak. To be fair to his tailor, *no* suit would have looked good on those rangy gorilla arms. His torso looked like he was smuggling a dozen hams under his shirt. Somewhere in there was a face, much scarred and afflicted with a badly considered mustache.

Zham stepped around the front of the bar, in the shadow of the balcony, and surveyed the thugs with a look that he hoped conveyed haughty disdain.

"I was a little busy," he said, waggling his eyebrows to imply he'd been up to mysterious business in the storage closet. "I hear you were looking for me?"

"Mr. Vargas is looking for you," the big brute corrected in that voice that made Zham's teeth buzz. "It would please him very much if you would drop by for a little chat."

Zham made a face. "I'm afraid my social calendar's a mess at the moment. I may be able to fit him in next month?"

"Mr. Vargas doesn't like waiting. He gets unhappy."

"I'm very sorry for him, but—"

"Keeping him happy is my job," the big man rumbled. "So, we'll just be going along now, shall we?"

The slightly less impressive thugs began to spread out, cutting off Zham's potential escape routes. He eyed them and gave an exasperated sigh.

"That's how it is, then? Six against one?" He snorted. "Well."

"Well *what?*" the brute growled.

"Nothing." Zham held up his hands, then inspected his cuffs. "Just thinking you must not be as tough as you look, if you need all your friends to take me."

There was a chilly silence. Then, blessedly, someone laughed up on the balcony. A few additional titters ran around the room. They stopped as the big man looked about.

"I don't need help to take you," he said. "I don't even need both *hands.*"

"Sure, sure." Zham gave an exaggerated wink. "Whatever you say, of course."

"You think you're very clever." The thug stepped closer, waving his companions back. "Lure me into a fight, is that it? One on one? Mano a mano?" He took another step, looming. "Well, now you've got one. Still seem like a good idea? Any other clever things to say?"

"Honestly, your breath makes me regret *all* my choices," Zham said. He squared off, raising what seemed in the moment like puny little fists. Very slowly, the thug's huge, scarred mitts came up as well. "Let's have a nice clean fight, and *Niko!*"

There was a ripping, crunching sound. Niko emerged from the nook, feet off the ground, hanging on the curtain with all her not-very-substantial weight. She swung in an arc a foot above the floor, like an extremely cautious swashbuckling hero.

The top of the curtain, it turned out, was tied to the balcony railing. While Niko was not particularly heavy, the miracle of leverage aided by the pressure of the onlookers above proved to be too much for the cheap wood. With a series of crunching snaps, a section of rail gave way, dumping Niko on her arse and raining splinters of wood and incautious bar patrons down on Zham and the thug.

Zham, for his part, threw himself backward over the bar, clearing a substantial part of it and sending several mugs to smash against the back wall. The thug, with no such warning, put up his arms to shield his face from flying splinters and was taken off guard by the screaming young woman who crushed his fedora and bore him to the ground. Several others followed, the big man's great bulk softening their falls and easing Zham's conscience a little.

"Niko!" he yelled. "Come on!"

The girl was quick; he had to give her that. She'd already popped to her feet, and by the time he'd wrenched open the back door, she was right behind him. They crossed a narrow office, hit another door full tilt, and emerged into a stinking alley lined with anonymous back entrances. The air was bracingly cold after the closeness of the tavern, and the Layer overhead was shredded, a few stars peeping through the blanket of moonlit cloud.

"How'd you know the railing would break?" Niko gasped out.

"I had to pay to fix it last time, didn't I?" Zham looked around frantically and pointed. "This way."

The alley continued only a little ways before making a dogleg back toward the main street. When Zham emerged, he was dismayed to see they were only half a block from the front door of the Lonely Bug, with several of the fedora'd thugs already out front. He hurriedly turned his back and started whistling, but increased shouting indicated that his attempt at casual nonchalance had not convinced anyone.

There were a few pedestrians about, late-night carousers mixing with the earliest of the early-morning trades. There were no cabs in sight, however, nor any of Aur Marka's Civil Guard in their spiked caps. Not that a guardsman would have been much help. Mr. Vargas presumably had plenty of friends there. But the presence of Authority might have bought a few minutes of not being beaten to a pulp. Instead, all that offered itself in the immediate vicinity was an old man unloading steaming loaves of bread from a cargo scooter.

A bass roar came from the door to the bar. "Get him!"

"Beggars and choosers, eh?" Zham said aloud.

He jogged to the scooter, gratified to find that the old man had left the keys in the ignition. Niko looked at him questioningly as he slid into the driver's seat.

"Get in!"

"But it's not yours," she said, forehead wrinkling in genuine confusion.

"It's wossname, military necessity." Zham raised his voice to address the old man, who'd just noticed them and started shouting. "We'll pay for it, I promise! Send the bill to the captain of the *Last Stop*!" Three of the thugs, led by the big man in the smashed hat, were only a dozen yards away. "Now, Niko!"

Niko bit her lip and threw herself in the back among the remaining bread pallets. Zham gunned the engine, which produced more of a gentle *put-put-put* than a satisfying roar, and pulled out into the street. The big thug saw them and started sprinting, but the scooter's ancient motor picked up speed and they quickly accelerated downslope toward the next tier. Zham glanced in the cracked mirror and flipped the bird over his shoulder, feeling very pleased with himself.

Lights came on in front of the bar. First one, then another, then four together. The deep rumble of *real* engines filled the road.

"Bloody *bugfuckers*," Zham growled, and hammered the accelerator. "Niko, hold on to something!"

The ancient city of Aur Marka, once second to only to Szacus as a shining beacon of Imperial glory (or so the locals insisted), clung to the side of its mountain like a tenacious bit of lichen. With no convenient shoulder or saddle of ground to build on, the people had been forced to hack out flat space from the living rock, tier after tier, turning the side of the mountain into a giant's staircase. At the top were the High Docks, where cargo was unloaded, its handlers getting assistance from gravity as they moved it first to the great markets and then to the Low Docks on the city's bottom tier, where other ships waited to haul it out across the Empire and beyond. Past the Low Docks there was only the gray mass of the city wall, with a lonely path running through the Hunter's Gate and down into the riotous green of the deadly lowlands.

The main up-down roads cut diagonally back and forth to keep a reasonable slope, switchbacking across the tiers. An observer at the corner of one of those switchbacks, by what was quickly becoming the gray light of morning, might have seen the following in sequence:

1. a cargo scooter, going faster than it was ever meant to and taking the corner tipped up on two of its three wheels, with a large man hunched ridiculously behind the tiny windscreen and a young woman in the back hurling a barrage of rolls from a half-empty pallet,

2. a motorcycle ridden by a large woman in a dark suit, hair flapping from under a recently lost fedora, in the process of wiping out due to being struck in the face by a ballistic pastry,

3. a second motorcycle, ridden by a large man in a dark suit, maintaining a determined pursuit, and

4. an enormous six-wheeled black car, with four blinding headlights and heavily tinted windows, accelerating to an unsafe speed and grinding buttery breakfast under its tires.

Whether there actually *were* any observers to see all this was not a question Zham could answer. His attention was entirely consumed by avoiding death. The indifferently paved Markan streets thumped and bumped underneath the scooter's threadbare tires, every rattle transmitting itself into a jerk of the miniature steering wheel.

"I got one!" Nico crowed, followed by a tremendous crunching, splattering sound. "Oof, right into the fruit stall. I hope she's okay."

"Let's focus on *us* being okay," Zham said. He felt a sudden, impossibly urgent need to pee. "Turn!"

This was the cue for Niko to put down her rolls and hold on for dear life as they crossed another tier and Zham yanked the scooter through a ninety-degree turn, slewing out nearly to the edge of the road. A bump sent them into the air for a moment of stomach-churning weightlessness, which brought an extended squeak from Niko and a shower of baked goods as the remainder of her ammunition leapt into the air. The scooter landed with a thud, Zham nearly bit through his tongue, and the tires squealed. Behind them, the second motorcyclist made the turn with considerably more elegance.

"You okay?" Zham shouted.

"There's no more rolls, Zham!" Niko said.

The biker gunned his engine and pulled up beside them, grabbing wildly for Niko with one hand. She snatched up a baguette that had fallen in the cargo bed and broke it over the thug's fedora in a shower of crumbs. He wobbled and dropped back but recovered quickly.

There was a deeper roar and the big car pulled in close behind them. Zham didn't recognize the make but it looked like one of those bulletproof Anark jobs, the sort of thing some TEC executive might take to work to foil snipers working for rival department heads. This close, the engine sounded like a continuous roll of thunder.

Niko frantically pressed herself against the front of the cargo bed just behind Zham, groping for another baguette and not finding one. The front of the car, protected by a gleaming steel bug-catcher, hit the back of the scooter with a *crunch*, shoving it forward and forcing Zham to fight wildly to maintain control.

"Do something!" Niko shouted.

"Hang on *tight*," Zham yelled back, and spun the wheel.

At the same time, his right hand yanked at a lever beside the seat. The scooter had a lev tank, a small steel sphere wrapped in engine tubing jammed awkwardly between the driver and the cargo bed. Inside it were a few cups of lev held in liquid form under pressure. The lever diverted fuel to the tank heater, which would rapidly heat the lev to a boil. Boiling lev meant levgas. Levgas meant levity, and the hotter it got the more it lifted. The tank would strain at its iron cage, trying to escape into the sky. The scooter, as a result, would be lighter and able to carry heavier loads.

Such was the theory, anyway. Zham doubted the baker had much use for the lev tank, so it was even money the whole thing was busted. He mouthed a quick prayer to any gods in the vicinity as the scooter tipped up on two wheels, screaming toward the entrance to a narrow lane.

Either the gods were kind or the baker was more into scooter maintenance than he seemed. Zham felt the lurch as the lev tank started taking the scooter's weight, keeping them tipped almost vertical long past the point where the thing should have flipped. He just made the turn into the lane, the left rear wheel spinning wildly in midair, only centimeters from scraping the brick wall. Zham slammed the lever back down, spun the wheel the other way, and shouted over his shoulder.

"Left, hang on the left side!"

Niko, all gods bless her, was quick on the uptake and threw herself over the raised rim of the cargo bed. As the lev cooled back into liquid, the scooter wobbled, wanting to continue its turn and flip over. Niko's weight, slender though it was, convinced it not to, and it slammed back onto the road with a bone-shaking thump. Small important parts broke free and bounced off merrily behind them with a metallic clatter.

"That was *awesome!*" Niko yelled.

Zham's knuckles were white on the undersized wheel. The irony did not escape him that an aero pilot used to speeds of hundreds of klicks was breathing hard at a lousy few dozen kph. On the other hand, he was usually a bit more than half a meter off the ground.

Behind them, there was a great squeal of brakes as the big car slewed to a halt. The motorcyclist skidded to a stop as well, shouted something to his companions, and gunned the motor to follow them down the lane.

Brick-fronted apartment buildings flashed past on both sides, a blur of flowers in window boxes and tasteful wrought-iron fences. A few early dog-walkers were out on the sidewalks, eyes going wide at the clattering scooter belching black smoke in furious gouts from its tailpipe. Thankfully, there were still no other vehicles on the road, but Zham had to swerve to avoid tipped-over garbage bins and the occasional parked car. The biker slalomed in pursuit, gaining fast.

"These guys *really* want to get you!" Niko said. "What did you do to them?"

"I borrowed a lot of money from their boss!" Zham shouted back.

"Just that?"

Zham made a face Niko couldn't see. "There might have been a thing with his granddaughter. But *she* came on to *me*, and— Shit!"

He yanked the wheel as the street reached an abrupt T junction, narrowly missing a collision with another scooter. Niko was thrown across the back with a whoop.

"Are you all right?" he said.

"Only mildly concussed so far," she shouted. "Is this all still part of the being-a-pilot lesson?"

Zham found a grin unaccountably spreading across his face. "This is more of the advanced course. But full marks so far!"

The biker was still on them but hanging a few lengths back, waiting for something. Zham made another turn and tried to recall anything about the map of Aur Marka. He'd been more interested in the location of potential watering holes than the street grid, but it could only be one more tier before they reached the Low Docks. All he had to do was head *down*.

Finally, the alleys met the switchbacking main street again, and he dodged a yapping terrier and broke out into the clear. The sun was rising, peeking through the Layer to paint the city streets with long shadows. A few other scooters and a delivery truck were on the road, but there was no sign of the biker or the armored car. Zham slowed the scooter's straining engine and made another turn, wondering if Vargas's goons had finally called it a day.

Of course they hadn't. This last turn put him on the last tier before the docks, the road a straight, sloping shot down to the broad cargo yard and the jutting piers beyond. He could see the *Last Stop*, a rectangular slab of battered gray that right now looked as enticing as the Cradle itself. Unfortunately, between him and the promised land, there was an obstacle.

The Low Docks were surrounded by a sturdy chain-link fence topped with an outward-sloping baffle and strung with razor wire. The main gate was wide open even this early in the morning, but the big black car was pulled up in front of it, blocking the way with all of its intimidating bulk. Three thugs crouched behind it, ready to leap out if Zham attempted to slip by on foot. Beyond them, on the other side of the gate, a quartet of dock security people looked on with interest.

The *blat* of an engine made him look over his shoulder. The biker was back, joined by his somewhat worse-for-wear companion. They sat in the middle of the street, poised for pursuit.

Niko pushed herself up on the lev tank to peer at the road in front of them and whistled. "Now what?"

"I'm thinking," Zham said, grinding his teeth.

There was a truck parked on the side of the road not far from the gate, its rear doors folded down into a ramp. When he shifted his head, it almost seemed to line up . . .

Niko followed his gaze, and her eyes went very wide. "Oh, no. You're kidding."

"Nope," Zham said, shifting gears and leaning on the accelerator.

"No way," Niko said, wind starting to whip around her. "No chance; it's too far—"

"Take this!" Zham pulled a metal flask from his coat and handed it over his shoulder. He rapped the bottom of it on the pipes leading to the lev tank, where there was a rubber twist-off cap. "When I tell you, pour it in there!"

"I'm going to die," Niko said wonderingly. "I always wondered how I would die, and apparently, it's going to be 'smashed into a pulp by a crazy person on a scooter.' It's a pretty cool death, but I really, *really* wish I'd had time to get—"

"*Niko!*"

"Yes!" she squeaked.

"Do you trust me?"

"Not at all!"

"Take the fucking flask anyway!"

She grabbed it and started unscrewing the cap. Zham returned his attention to the truck, which was coming up fast. *Very* fast. Possibly no ancient cargo scooter had ever achieved such a speed. People on both sides of the street were pointing. Someone screamed.

The accelerator scarcely mattered now; the slope had taken over. Zham yanked the lev tank lever as far as it would go and fought the increasingly hard jerks of the wheel.

"*Now*, Niko!"

He didn't have time to look back and see if she did it or not. The truck was *right there*, its metal ramp contracting in his vision to the size of a pinhead, the scooter was fighting like a furious mantid, and he had to line it up *just right*—

Corrugated metal clattered beneath him. Zham felt them start to lose traction even before the wheels left the ramp, and the scooter *flew*.

You couldn't just *fly* with a scooter lev tank, obviously. It wasn't designed for it, couldn't stand the strain. The lev tank heater, even at full blast, couldn't get close to bringing the levgas to the furious heat it would need to carry the scooter's full weight. But—for the sake of argument—if some maniac had opened the maintenance cap and poured in a flask of bugblood extract, the purest uncut stuff, then possibly—

The scooter cleared the front of the truck and, impossibly, kept rising, laughing at the parabola dictated by mere gravity that would have deposited it into the fence with a horrible *crunch*. It rose until the wheels spun above the razor wire, passing over the heads of the astonished fedora thugs.

The machinery around the lev tank was making horrible, distressed noises. A part of the base of the tank began to glow cherry red. Zham worked the lever the other way but it made no difference, not with the fury of a thousand mantids already burning in the tubes. A rivet gave way with a sound like a gunshot.

The ground was really quite far away now. They were over the fence, past the guards. Below was a sea of heavy burlap sacks, ready for loading into some fat-bellied merchantman. Whatever was in them, it was likely to be softer than rock.

"Jump!" he screamed.

"What—" Niko started to say, then gave a rising whoop as Zham stood up in the driver's seat, grabbed her arms, and yanked her out of the cargo bed and over the side. He went with her, tumbling wildly, contorting himself to put her on top.

Above them, rising in glory like some solar divinity, the scooter reached its apotheosis. The lev tank exploded with such violence that the whole machine was torn in half, pieces of snarling metal whipping in every direction. A whistling fragment zipped past Zham's head, taking the tiniest nick out of his ear. He tightened his arms around Niko and squeezed his eyes shut.

Impact, with a *whuff* like a stove igniting. Pieces of scooter were falling from the sky with metallic *clang*s and *thud*s. Shouts and screams.

And then it seemed to be over. Zham opened his eyes and found himself inside a billowing white cloud. Flour tickled his nose, and he sneezed.

"Niko?" he said. "Are you all right?"

"Nope," she said, lying sprawled on his chest. "I'm definitely dead. See?" She raised her head, skin caked white with flour. "I'm a ghost!"

Zham blinked. Niko broke down in giggles, rolling off him to spread-eagle on more flour sacks.

"Okay," she said. "I'm updating my status to *moderately* concussed. Are we safe now?"

"Probably," Zham said weakly. He waved toward a gray shape slowly becoming visible through the thinning cloud of flour. "That's my ship. Welcome to the *Last Stop*."

CHAPTER TWO

Zham was bruised, scraped, bleeding from one ear, covered in flour, and somewhere on the strange littoral of early morning where the buzz hasn't quite worn off but the hangover is already starting to kick in. Even the muted sunlight coming in through the big windows that ringed *Last Stop*'s bridge was enough to make him narrow his eyes, and something at the base of his skull throbbed in time with his heartbeat.

Niko stood beside him, a small pile of flour gathering around her feet as it sifted down from the folds of her coat. If Quedra had noticed that she was there, she'd given no sign of it thus far, her attention being entirely taken up by her wayward brother.

Quedra Sa-Yool had a way of occupying most of the space in any room she entered. This was not because of her physical presence but in spite of it. She was a small woman, a bit broader than Niko but only a little taller, with the same dusky skin and epicanthic eyes as Zham himself. Her hair was straight where his was curly, and she kept it tied back in a Navy-precise ponytail rather than Zham's loose mop. She sat in a tall chair behind *Last Stop*'s plotting table. Only one of her canes leaned against the armrest, which told Zham that this was one of her better days. Not, of course, that you would guess that from her expression.

At her shoulder stood Martin Felder, the ship's XO, in a gray semi-uniform that contrasted with his very dark skin. He wore square-rimmed glasses and a studied lack of expression. Zham wasn't sure he'd ever seen the man smile, or for that matter frown.

"How many calls have we had, Martin?" Quedra said after an excruciating silence.

"Twenty-three, ma'am." As if on cue, the ship-to-shore phone jangled. "Twenty-four."

"And how many were from the Civil Guard?"

"Five. And a sixth from the Lord Mayor's office."

"It's a good thing we were about to leave anyway," Zham said.

"Has it occurred to you that we might need to come back?" Quedra said. "Did that enter into your calculations at all?"

"Can't say that it did," Zham said. He scratched the back of his head. "I was mostly trying to keep myself in one piece."

"Of course you were." She closed her eyes for a moment, as though summoning all her strength. "It's a miracle nobody was killed."

"It's a miracle *I* wasn't killed," Zham said.

"And these people who chased you? What did they want?"

"Misunderstanding about a bill."

"Of course it was."

"Speaking of, there's a baker who I promised we'd pay for use of his scooter—"

"Oh, he's been in touch," Quedra said. "Along with a number of others. Where exactly did you leave his scooter, by the way?"

"Down in the cargo yard. Sort of . . . generally around the place."

Niko gave a snort of suppressed laughter. Quedra's narrowed eyes flicked to her.

"This is Niko Fanucci," Zham put in. "Our new pilot. If she's half as good with an aero as she is with a baguette, we'll be glad to have her."

Another laugh from Niko, who furiously tried and failed to straighten her face.

"It's good to have you, Ms. Fanucci," Quedra said. "I apologize for my brother nearly getting you killed on your first day." She looked back at Zham. "And for his being out drinking when he ought to have been picking you up."

"Sorry, *ma'am!*" Zham said, clicking his heels and snapping a Navy salute. "I'll be sure to do my future drinking alone in the middle of the day, as is proper."

"That's *enough*," Quedra growled. "Get off my damned bridge."

Zham turned, back military-straight, and march-stepped to the door.

"It's a pleasure to meet you, ma'am," Niko said awkwardly, and hurried after him.

In the stairwell outside, Zham gripped the rail and tried to breathe, flaking paint digging into his palms. He stared unseeing at Aur Marka, spots of sun shifting across its buildings like a leopard's spots as the Layer churned high above. When Niko touched his shoulder, he practically jumped out of his shoes.

"Sorry," she said.

He shook his head. "*I'm* sorry. I hope I didn't put you in an awkward position back there."

"You absolutely did," Niko said cheerfully. "But that's a thing that happened and we'll all have to live with it." She looked sidelong at him. "I take it you and the captain don't get along?"

"The *captain* and I do fine," Zham muttered. "It's my sister I can't handle."

"Ah." Niko flapped her coat, dislodging a little more flour. "So. Not that your family relations aren't fascinating, but what exactly should I do now?"

"Do?" Zham blinked and returned his focus to the present. "Right, of course. You sent your stuff ahead?"

Niko nodded. "Such as it is."

"Then let's find your bunk. I'll give you the tour on the way down."

Last Stop's conning tower was a stubby thing, so they only had three flights of stairs to descend to reach the flight deck. It was not,

Zham had to admit, an impressive sight, unless you were into featureless expanses of metal with patchy gray paint. *Last Stop* was a four-tanker, a reliable if uninspired design with four primary lev tanks at the corners of a squat rectangle. From a distance, it looked like a gray box with a little poky bit sprouting from one side, the front corners rounded off in a vague concession to aerodynamics.

At the rear, a square bite from the edge of the flight deck marked the elevator to the hangar. Beside the conning tower was the ship's only real weapon, a dual 1.3 cm machine-gun mount set in a rotating ring turret like an ugly wart. A large figure in a tank top and canvas trousers was working on it, lowering a new box of ammunition into an open deck panel. She looked up as Zham approached and gave a grunt of greeting, then frowned on seeing Niko.

"Hey, Inge," Zham said. "This is Niko, the new pilot. Niko, this is Ingeborg. Shipboard security. She does shooting people and hitting things."

Ingeborg gave another approving grunt. She was as tall as Zham, heavyset and well-muscled. In a suit and fedora, she'd have blended in with Vargas's thugs, but Zham had never seen her wear anything more formal than a jumpsuit. Her pale skin was splotchy with sunburns, and her platinum blonde hair was woven into a heavy braid that hung halfway down her back. When she spoke, her voice was surprisingly melodious.

"Also, I break things." She looked over at Zham. "She hard on you?"

There was no need to specify which *she*. Zham waggled his palm in a so-so gesture.

Ingeborg snorted. "Must be your lucky day."

"Have you seen Aoife and Lanzo?"

"Down on the cargo deck with Karl."

"Nice to meet you!" Niko said as they walked away. Ingeborg grunted again and waved without looking up from her work.

"She's friendly, I promise," Zham said. "Just not very talkative."

A recessed stairway led down to the hangar deck, its cavernous expanse running the length of the ship. A mad fresco of colored lines stenciled on the floor marked off various parking configurations, but only four aircraft were currently stored there, the rest of the space gradually filling with miscellaneous refuse. Looking around with fresh eyes, Zham felt instantly embarrassed at the mass of peeling paint and rusting fixtures. Half the bare bulbs hanging from the ceiling were burnt out, lending the whole place a shadowy, sepulchral quality.

Niko noticed none of this. She had eyes only for the aeros, stepping forward with the reverence of a pilgrim arriving at a long-promised shrine. These, at least, were well looked after. On a levship like *Last Stop*, almost everything could break down except the lev tanks themselves, and the vessel wouldn't fall out of the sky. But an aero was always one breakdown away from disaster.

Closest to them was Zham's own machine, the DeFerra-111, its body painted a dark green with a jaunty angled red stripe around the nose. Watching Niko stare, Zham took a moment to admire the aero as a sleek airborne predator, the slight sweep to its wings and the raked bubble cockpit. Normally, he saw it more as an amalgamation of potentially faulty parts or a collection of behaviors and quirks, like the need to double-crank the landing gear lever or the janky artificial horizon. It was far from the worst thing Zham had ever flown, but far from the best, either.

From the expression on Niko's face, though, it was as though the fighter had descended from the heavens covered in glory. Zham abruptly remembered being sixteen, when his big sister had wangled him a private tour of a Navy corvette. He wondered if his eyes had been as wide as Niko's were now.

There was a giggle, and a waterfall of brown hair appeared, hanging down under the 111's starboard wing. It was followed by a small face, upside-down.

"Hey, Anni," Zham said, crouching.

"I'm Elli, *actually*," the girl said. She slithered further down the wing, then dismounted with a forward flip that left her on her feet with arms spread and a pleased expression on her face. "Dad said you got in *trouble*."

"Big trouble!" another piping voice chimed in. Anni's head appeared over the edge of the port wing.

Zham decided he would rather not get into that with a pair of tweens, and pushed Niko forward as a distraction. "Come down and meet our new pilot!"

"Hiya!" Niko said brightly. "Are you guys supposed to be playing on the aeros?"

Elli sniffed. "We were checking the flap bearings, *actually*."

"Zham doesn't clean them enough, so they get rusty!" Anni slid off the wing, her dismount only a little less graceful than her sister's. The twins were eleven, pale and freckled like Niko, and both wore stained gray jumpsuits with rolled-up cuffs and goggles pushed up onto their foreheads.

"They do maintenance?" Niko said.

"Apparently," Anni said, in a gruff and not entirely inaccurate imitation of her father, "no one else is going to!"

"Is she going to fly the S-1?" Elli said.

"Her name is Niko, and yes, I think so," Zham said.

"Dad says it's a stupid piece of shit," Anni chimed in.

"And a death trap," Elli added.

"He says that about everything," Zham said to Niko. "According to Karl, the whole ship is always one dropped wrench away from going up in a huge fireball."

"*Boom!*" Niko shouted unexpectedly, setting off a round of giggling from the girls.

"*Boom!*"

"*Boom!*"

"Is your dad around here?"

Anni pointed across the hangar, still engaged in making explosion noises. Niko was crouched down to their height and waving her arms frantically, to further laughter. Zham pulled her away as she mugged wide-eyed shock in their direction.

"You're comfortable around kids, I take it," Zham said.

"I have sisters," Niko said. "Do they really work on the aeros?"

He nodded. "Karl keeps them in line, more or less."

"More or less?"

"Nothing's gone boom *yet*."

Ahead was the Krager-7a, the largest of their little squadron and the only twin-engine, with a pair of silver-painted propellers bracketing its nose cone. Karl, Aoife, and Lanzo were gathered under its wing, peering at one of the ordnance hardpoints.

As a trio, they did not have a lot in common. Karl looked much the same as his girls, only taller and dad-lier, with a neatly trimmed beard and his own pair of goggles around his neck. Lanzo was shorter and swarthier, hair slicked back and gleaming, dressed in a natty civilian suit. Aoife, beside him, was a head taller and considerably broader in the shoulders, an impression enhanced by an intricate, wide-skirted Szacine dress in dark red and black that looked as out of place in an airplane hangar as oily rags in a grand ballroom.

"The prodigal returns!" Karl said.

"The way Quedra was blowing smoke, I'm surprised your ears aren't burned black," Lanzo said.

"Only lightly singed," Zham said. "I'm showing our new recruit around. Everyone, this is Niko. Niko, this is the rest of the squadron and the guy who keeps us in the air."

"Nicolosa Fanucci," Niko said, with a slight bow. "Glad to be aboard."

"Most welcome," Lanzo said, a broad smile spreading across his face. He bowed low, and for a moment Zham thought he was going to try to kiss Nico's hand. "Of course, I imagine a woman of your quality is welcome anywhere."

"Oh, shut it," Aoife said in her lilting accent. She stuck out her hand for Niko to shake. "You'll learn to ignore him, I promise. Gods know I have."

"Your dress is lovely," Niko said, diplomatically changing the subject. "What's the occasion?"

"Who needs an occasion to look fine?" Aoife gave a little twirl. "Besides, if I waited till it was *appropriate*, I'd never wear anything except ratty underwear and T-shirts stained with engine grease, like this one." She hooked a finger at Zham, who held up his hands defensively.

"I have other shirts," he said. "I'm wearing one right now!"

"Looks like you were in a bakery explosion, too," Aoife said.

"That's not *entirely* inaccurate," Niko said.

"What did you destroy this time?" Karl said.

"Long story," Zham said. "And we're about to collapse with exhaustion, so—"

"I think I'm getting a second wind, actually," Niko said brightly.

"*I'm* about to collapse, so I'd like to please get her downstairs." Zham took a breath. "Aoife, did you clean out S—the, ah, stuff from her room?"

Aoife nodded, her face going serious for a moment. "I put her bag down there, too."

"Thank you," Zham said. "Come on, Niko; you'll have plenty of time to gossip with this lot."

"I still want to know what exploded," Karl said.

"And I would be happy to hear the story as well, my lovely," Lanzo said.

"Later!" Niko said with a wave as she followed Zham back to the staircase. The twins, who'd been watching from behind a wheel strut, skittered out of the way in a storm of laughter.

"What do you think?" Zham said.

"I admit it's not *exactly* what I expected when I pictured a mercenary company," Niko said. "But literally nothing about this evening has gone as I expected, so that's about par for the course."

"It's not a bad crew, all told. If Lanzo bothers you, tell him to back off and he'll steer clear. Quedra's made that *very* explicit to him."

"He reminds me of my Uncle Paolo," Niko said. "Mother used to hit him with a ladle when he whistled. Does Aoife always dress like that?"

"Except when she's in the cockpit. She claims to have missed her calling as a Szacine princess."

"By about a century, I should think."

"Here." Zham indicated a doorway. "This is you."

The third level of the *Last Stop* was mostly given over to crew quarters and the mess. Long hallways, irregularly lit, were lined with doors on both sides. The room the twins shared had color splashed across the door, depicting what was either a unicorn or some kind of mutant dog. The rest were anonymous, marked only by flaking gray paint chips.

"That's a lot of rooms," Niko said, looking down to the end of the hall. "Where is everybody?"

"Most of them we use for storage," Zham said. "You've pretty much met the crew, except for Sev. They're the ship's engineer; they more or less live down on the engine deck."

"That's really it?"

Zham shrugged uncomfortably. "We'd have more if this were a proper warship. For the kinds of missions we fly, it's usually enough."

Niko accepted that with a nod and opened the door. The rooms were small and spare, with a desk, a chair, and a bunk hanging on the wall, folded up when not in use. A black duffel bag sat on the desk.

"That's all your stuff?" Zham said.

"I travel light," Niko said, unzipping it and rummaging around.

"The bunks can be a little stiff," Zham said. "You just have to lean on it a little—there."

"What're those?" Niko said.

Several photos hung on the wall by the side of the bunk. Zham frowned at them, then pulled them down.

"Nothing," he muttered. "Previous occupant's stuff."

"Is that her?" Niko said, pointing to the last one before Zham grabbed it. "Next to you?"

"Yeah." Zham jammed the pictures in his pocket and turned away abruptly. "Sorry. Headache's starting to get to me."

"Go rest. I can take it from here." Niko waved him out the door. "Thanks for the tour."

"I'll show you the rest later." Zham yawned as he stumbled out. "We'll have plenty of time."

Niko's door closed. Zham stood in the hall for a moment. His hand clenched into a fist, and the photos crumpled around his fingers.

By the time Zham woke up, with the dry-mouthed, curried-eyeball feeling only the finest of hangovers could provide, *Last Stop* was in the air.

The ship's engines, even muffled by a layer of decking, were a subliminal throbbing presence in every metallic surface. But even without them, Zham would have known they were above the Layer. The air *tasted* different in a way that was hard to describe.

He went through his morning ablutions and chewed dry cereal and toast alone in the mess, the big space feeling especially cavernous with no one else around. The other pilots would be up in the hangar or on the flight deck, enjoying the view. Quedra would be on the bridge, staring down at the map table with narrowed eyes and waiting for Zham to join her so she could subject him to cold looks and clipped annoyance.

Zham, therefore, went in the opposite direction, down a narrow metal stair to the engine deck. The air grew perceptibly warmer as he descended, hot and dry like the breath of an oven. The constant thrum of machinery grew louder. The lights down there were dimmer and red-tinted, helping to spare the eyes of the sole occupant.

"Sev?" Zham called out.

He'd learned long ago it was better not to wander far down there. Away from the fore-and-aft corridor, the place was an incomprehensible tangle of pipes, tubes, and humming machines, patches layered on jury-rigs layered on temporary expedients that had never ended. That *Last Stop* flew at all was testimony to Sev's genius.

"Kid," a gravelly voice said behind him. Zham had expected it but he still jumped. Sev walked like a cat.

The engineer was roughly spherical in shape, with stubby legs and no visible neck thanks to several overlapping fur collars drawn up over their chin. Zham had no idea how much of their apparent bulk was layers of coats; Sev claimed to take a chill easily and was never seen without them, all covered over with a black rubberized overcoat that flapped around their ankles. Their hands were swathed in thick canvas work gloves pitted with shiny burns. The overcoat had a hood, which Sev kept drawn up over their ears, and heavy goggles covered their eyes. About all that was visible of their skin was a bulbous, peeling nose sticking over the top of their collar.

"Hey," Zham said, affecting nonchalance.

Sev cocked their head, giving him a knowing look. "Hiding from your sister again?"

Zham hesitated, then gave a mute nod.

Sev gave a grunt. "I've got some tea brewing."

The engineer beckoned and stumped off, their rocking, waddling gait belying a considerable turn of speed. Zham had no idea how old Sev actually was—they'd *seemed* old when they first met, back in the Navy more than a decade earlier—but the years hadn't hurt the engineer's agility. Zham had to work to keep up, ducking to fit through low doorways and edging around clanging, sweating pipes.

In a little nook tucked amidst the shadowy machinery, there was a table covered in a black-and-white checked cloth, tinted crimson by the light. It had two chairs, a teapot sitting atop a complicated heating engine, and a silver tray in the shape of a curled-up cat set with shortbread cookies. Zham had no idea where Sev got these, since they never left the ship.

He took the visitor's chair, and Sev eased into their own shorter, wider seat. As was customary for these little chats, Zham took a cookie and waited in silence while the engineer went through the ritual of pouring the tea, adding cream to one cup and sugar to the other, and stirring both. Zham took the sweetened one, blew across the top, and took a sip, then bit into the cookie. Sev pushed their collar down with one hand and brought the cup to their lips.

"How's the ship?" Zham said after a decent interval.

"Held together with chewing gum and baling wire," Sev said. They had a voice like a chain smoker, raspy as a buzz saw. "Same as always."

"She likely to fall apart before we get to Aur Lunach?"

"S'pose not." It sounded like Sev was smiling behind their collar, but Zham could never be sure. These exchanges were also part of the ritual. "So, what's eating you, kid?"

"You heard what happened yesterday?"

Sev nodded. In spite of never coming abovedecks, they always seemed to know everything that went on aboard ship.

"Impressed you made it," they said. "Using pure extract to goose the lev tank was ballsy. Coulda gone bad."

"It nearly did," Zham admitted. "Quedra gave me an earful."

"Ain't the first time," Sev said. "Won't be the last, either, I'd bet."

"Probably not."

Sev took a long drink from their tea and set it down. "Who was it that was after you?"

"Vargas."

"He the one you get those parts from?"

Zham nodded.

"You should tell her, kid."

"Why?" Zham said bitterly. "So she can tear me another new orifice? I can square with Vargas with the pay from this job."

"Doubt it'll be that much," Sev said. "Number three tank's losing pressure. Needs to be drained and resealed, and that'll cost. Can't put it off much longer."

"Bugshit," Zham swore. Figures ran through his mind, but the amounts seemed to melt into one another. Math had never been his strong suit.

"With payouts like we've been getting, it's barely worth putting this heap in the air," Sev said. "Spend more on repairs than we take in, even if nobody pokes any holes in us."

"We need better jobs," Zham said. His jaw tightened. "You have to tell her."

"You know she doesn't listen to me, kid," Sev said gently. "Not anymore."

"But—"

"Better money means more risk, and she won't do it. Sam was the last straw—"

"Don't fucking talk to *me* about Sam," Zham said. There was a pause, and he let out a tight breath. "Sorry. You're right. But we can't go on like this. Sooner or later, even you won't be able to keep *Last Stop* flying, and then . . ."

And then *what*? Zham honestly didn't know. The thought of Quedra without a ship to command felt *unnatural*, as strange as imagining her without a nose. She could no more just give up and do something else than Zham could quit piloting aeros or stop breathing.

"So, talk to her," Sev said.

"You think she listens to *me*?"

"More than anyone else. You're her brother."

"Her screw-up little brother. She doesn't trust me to do anything except fly."

Sev sipped their tea. "Why does she trust you to fly?"

Zham blinked, blindsided. Eventually, he ventured, "Because I'm good at it?"

"Are you good at anything else?"

"Of course." Zham reddened. "I like to think so, anyway."

"Does she *know* that? Has she seen it?"

Zham opened his mouth to reply and fell silent. Sev sighed.

"Quedra carries a heavy load," they said.

"I *know* that. If she'd share it a little, we'd all be better off—"

"She doesn't dare. Like you said, she doesn't trust anybody unless she's sure of what they can do."

"If you've got a point, please tell me," Zham said, rubbing his temples. "I'm too hungover for games."

Sev shifted and set down their empty teacup. "If you want her to listen to you, you gotta show her you're trustworthy."

"How can I do that if she doesn't trust me to handle anything?"

"It's a bit of a knot, I admit. But you gotta figure it out." Sev half-rolled out of their chair. "Getting chased through town on a burning scooter after a bender probably ain't it. That's some free advice right there."

"Didn't have much choice," Zham said, but without much bite. He chewed his lip, lost in thought.

"You can find your own way up, I expect," Sev said. "I hear pump number four's gone off again. 'Scuse me."

Zham gave a distracted nod and took another cookie.

CHAPTER
THREE

A week passed. *Last Stop* joined up with her charges, a trio of broken-down bulk freighters from Aur Garerra making the run south to Aur Lunach and wary of pirates flying out of the wilds. *Last Stop* trailed the cargo ships and sent up two-plane patrols, which meant long, boring days in a cramped cockpit or waiting around.

Zham and Niko were in the waiting phase, standing on the flight deck as Aoife and Lanzo maneuvered for a landing. Zham was engaged in his usual battle to convince himself he didn't have to pee again *already*, while Niko played tag with Anni and Elli, chasing them around and under the S-1's landing gear. A stiff breeze over the bow combined with *Last Stop*'s own speed to produce a wind strong enough to wring tears from ungoggled eyes and set scarves to flapping.

A week was long enough that Zham was getting used to the view again. Too much time on the ground always made him forget how *big* it seemed up here and how bright it could get without the Layer to dim the sun. Now the Layer was below them, an unbroken blanket of white clouds stretching as far as the eye could see in any direction, and the sun was shining in its full unshrouded brilliance atop a cerulean blue sky. A few shredded clouds drifted even higher overhead—those would be pure water vapor, rather than the mix of water and levgas that made up the Layer—but they did nothing to provide shade. *Last Stop*'s shadow looked sharp and angular on the rolling mass of the Layer, only a few ship-lengths below, and they left a long white wake like twin snakes unspooling behind them.

Overhead, Zham heard the drone of engines over the whistle of the wind. Moments later, he spotted two black specks closing rapidly from astern, flashing with green recognition lights. The first grew rapidly into Aoife's 7a, the big fighter-bomber coming in straight and level with landing gear deployed. It passed over their heads in a rush of wind and noise—the girls shouted at the top of their lungs, arms waving—and touched down, bouncing once before coming to a stop. Aoife taxied to one side to clear the deck for Lanzo's smaller Mercurio. Lanzo waggled the wings for the girls (and Niko, who joined in the shouting) before bringing his aero to a neat halt.

Aoife was already out of the cockpit, striding across the deck and pulling her scarf away so her long brown hair streamed in the wind. For a woman who regularly wore the height of centuries-old fashion, she was remarkably comfortable in a baggy, shapeless flight suit and a leather jacket as well.

"See anything?" Niko called.

"Clear skies," Aoife said. "Most excitement was when one of the merchies started belching smoke, then stopped again."

"Mechanical issue?" Zham said.

"More likely somebody left lunch on the stove too long," Aoife said. "Either way, it's not our problem." She clapped Zham on the shoulder. "Good luck. Here's to another quiet day, eh?"

"Getting tired of quiet, myself," Lanzo called out. "A little action to stir up the blood is what we need."

"I'll stir your bloody blood for you if you don't let them get on with it," Aoife said. Lanzo mimed shock but followed her off the deck.

"Bloody blood, bloody bloody blood!" Elli called out, and Anni picked up the chorus.

"Are those two—" Niko waved at the departing pilots and raised her eyebrows. "You know. Together? They sound like an old married couple."

"Not at the moment," Zham said. "Every six months or so, Lanzo wears Aoife down and they try it for about two weeks before she loses patience."

"Hmm." If Zham was any judge, Niko was looking speculatively at Aoife's retreating back.

"Come on," Zham said, clapping her on the shoulder. "We've got hours of nothing to look forward to."

Prepping for takeoff was as automatic as tying his shoes, and Zham could let his mind wander as his hands tapped and tested the gauges and controls. He settled his helmet and plugged the comm line into its socket. The faint hiss of white noise filled his ears.

"Zham, ready to go," he said into the throat mike. The missing formality of the Navy, the signs and countersigns that went with takeoff, itched like a phantom limb. "Clear?"

"Clear," Quedra's voice crackled in his ears.

"Niko?"

Her cheerful voice was shot with static. "All set!"

Zham punched the autoignition switch, and the engine coughed and spat dark smoke before evening out. Another automatic check of the gauges—plenty of bugblood in the tanks, a full load of 1.3 cm just in case, oil and hydraulic pressure and a dozen other things. His feet flexed on the rudder pedals.

"Here I go, then," he said.

The engine went from a purr to a roar. The 111 eased forward onto the flight strip. As he turned toward the bow, the wind caught the wings, making the aero rock as though it were ready to leap into the air of its own accord. Zham smiled to himself.

"I know the feeling," he muttered, and pushed the throttle forward.

Taking off from a ship in flight was easier, in some sense, than doing it from the ground. The air was thicker down below the Layer, but up here, there was a lot more room for error. If you went off the end of the runway, there were no houses to plow into, just thousands of meters of open sky. Still, Zham made it a point of pride not to let his undercarriage dip below *Last Stop*'s flight deck. His right hand pulled back on the stick, and the 111 climbed with a growl, arcing smoothly up and away.

Below him, the white-and-blue-painted S-1 followed just as neatly. Niko could indeed fly, as Vanta had promised. Zham had held his breath when she'd tried her first landing—*that* was the tricky part—but she'd parked the little fighter as easily as if it were a motorcar. Whether she could *shoot* was an open question but not one that was likely to be answered today.

Zham led her into a spiraling climb, gaining altitude until *Last Stop* was a tiny gray rectangle trailing its long, snaky wake. The three cargo freighters were stubby spears at the tips of their own white trails, and below them the Layer went on and on, only a handful of broken patches giving fleeting glimpses of the ground far, far below.

"What's the plan, flight leader?" Niko said. "Anything exciting on deck?"

"I was thinking," Zham drawled, "of hours of flying in circles and pissing in jars."

The S-1's wings waggled playfully. "Way ahead of you."

"I spy with my little eye," Niko said, "something beginning with *c*."

"Clouds," Zham groaned.

"You're good at this!"

"It was clouds the last seventeen times."

"I'm trying to psych you out. Is it working?"

"Yes."

"Awesome. Your turn."

"I'm not taking another turn. I'm never taking another turn again."

"Aw." Niko was silent for a blessed moment. "Now what?"

"If you're going to be a pilot," Zham said, "you really need to build up your tolerance for boredom."

"Noted. Can we play truth or dare?"

"Dares sound like a really bad idea under the circumstances."

"Better pick truth, then."

"No."

Another pause. "I spy—"

"All *right*," Zham said. "What do you want know?"

"Who's the girl?"

"What girl?"

"The one who was with you in that photo. She was on the crew, right? Nobody talks about her."

Zham thumbed his mike off and took a few breaths.

"Are you always this nosy?" he said eventually.

"Always," she said cheerfully. "My mom told me it was going to get me in big trouble someday."

"If nobody talks about it, have you considered that's because they don't want to?"

"I get it," Niko said more quietly. "But it's hard being the only one who doesn't know something, right? It's like there's pits all around me I can't see."

That, Zham had to admit, was fair. They'd brought Niko in to be a part of the crew. That meant they owed her something.

"Her name is—" He stopped himself, swallowed. "*Was* Sam. Samantha. She was a pilot. It's her room you're in."

Niko was quiet a moment. "She died?"

"She died." Zham heard a voice in the back of his mind, pushed it away. "It's always a risk when you're a sell-stick, but we don't always . . . think about it."

"Can I ask what happened? Was it in action?"

Zham really, really wished she hadn't. But there was nothing for it now. "Of a sort. Mantid swarm."

"Oh."

He closed his eyes for a moment. "Some of that glop they spit got in her engine and she lost power. We were low, under the Layer, fighting—it doesn't matter. She couldn't bail out with so many mantids in the air, but she managed to get the aero down and land in a jungle clearing. She was hoping we could get to her with a descender, but . . . the mantids got there first."

"Oh, no."

She'd been stuck in her cockpit, mantids on all sides climbing on the wings of her Vdeka, their saliva etching the canopy. Her landing had been perfect, everything still in working order, including the radio. They'd all heard the clicks and squeals and breaking glass.

"*Tell Zham,*" she'd said, forced cheer masking a sob in her voice, "*that I wish he'd asked me out sometime.*"

Then a pistol shot, and insect sounds until the radio died.

Zham was barely aware of the long silence until Niko spoke again.

"Hey," she said. "Uh. I spy with my little eye something beginning with *p.*"

"I'm not going to fucking guess, Niko," Zham snapped.

"Then just look at ten o'clock low," Niko said.

"Why?" Zham had to push his goggles up to wipe his eyes. "What's there?"

"I can't be *sure,*" she said, "but I *think* the answer is *pirates.*"

There were four of them, in two pairs a few hundred meters apart, coming in at an angle to the cargo ships' course. Zham couldn't identify their aeros from his high altitude, but they were all single-engine fighters, which meant a mothership somewhere nearby. Their markings were a nondescript gray. If they'd seen him and Niko, they gave no sign of it.

"What do we do?" Niko said.

Zham chewed his lip, all thoughts of the past thankfully driven from his mind. Strictly speaking, what he ought to do was challenge them to state their business. But that would give away that he was there, and the odds of a squad of fighters being up there for anything *other* than nefarious purposes were low.

"If they *are* pirates," he said, unconsciously lowering his voice as though the intruders could overhear, "then when they get close enough, they'll have to—"

"Merchant convoy!" a woman's voice crackled on a general band. "We are armed and closing. Kill your engines and vent lev if you want to stay in one piece."

Any ship that obeyed that command would drift helplessly down to the Layer, a sitting duck for any vessel above them, at which point the pirate mothership would move in and send over a boarding party. But a lumbering cargo freighter with at best a couple of machine guns for self-defense had little choice; even a lightly armed fighter could tear it to shreds.

Which is where the sell-sticks came in. Zham punched for the base band.

"Quedra, did you hear this?"

"Just a bunch of chatter from the merchies," she snapped. "What's happening?"

"Bad guys. I'm going in. Get Aoife and Lanzo up as soon as you can."

"Zham—"

He clicked back to Niko. "Time to earn that paycheck. Ready?"

"Ready!" She gave a laugh with a touch of hysteria. "Question: is it normal to feel my heart trying to erupt from my ribs?"

"Perfectly. Take the one on the right on the first dive, then stay on my wing like Vanta taught you. You'll be fine.

"Right. Wing. Fine. Right. Wing. Fine."

"Here we go."

Zham winged over into a gentle dive, watching his rearview mirror until he was sure Niko had followed. The altimeter wound one way, the speedometer crept the other, the 111 starting to shiver and jolt with the violence of speed. Niko kept close—no mean feat of flying, given the difference in aeros—and Zham put her out of his mind.

Two of the pirate aeros were growing ahead, slowly at first and then abruptly too fast. Zham's target was cruising down the length of the cargo freighter, waiting for the merchies to respond to the challenge, still unawares. The aero was dead center in the deflector sight, growing until it filled the circle—

He thumbed the button on the control column, and six Haviari GS 1.3 cm machine guns chattered to life, two in each wing and two synchronized to fire through the 111's propeller. They were slightly angled to converge at three hundred meters, so six arcing threads of brilliant red tracers seemed to reach out for the pirate like a grasping hand. Sixty rounds a second spattered against the aero's gray-painted fuselage and chewed into the wing root like demented steel woodpeckers.

Then he was past, still screamingly fast, headed down toward the Layer. In his rearview he saw the pirate's wing break apart, pieces scattering as the body of the aero rolled over into a downward spiral. Niko was still with him, and the pirate's wingman was pulling into a frantic climb, trailing gouts of black smoke.

"Hoooooooly shit," Niko said, "holy bugfucking shit, I hit him, did you see, I fucking—"

"Steady," Zham said, "stay with me."

"Yeah, absolutely, I'm a supercool pilot who takes this in stride and I'm definitely not absolutely losing my shit—"

The Layer was coming up fast, masses of churning cloud. Zham craned his neck for the other two pirates, who'd been on the opposite side of the freighter. At first, he could see only one of the pair, heading away from the convoy in a long, shallow dive. Then he spotted the other maneuvering to come down after him.

"Niko!"

"Yes!"

"One's bugging out, but the other one wants to tangle. I'll pull up; you go down into the cloud and wait for my signal."

"Got it!"

Zham eased the stick back and the 111 levelled out. Niko's S-1 kept falling, plunging into the twisted mix of air and lev that made up the Layer. It was murky and unpleasant to fly in there but not actually *dangerous* unless the Layer mounded up into one of its rare lightning storms.

The pirate was above and behind him, trying for the same high-side pass Zham had used to down his companion. He was having difficulty, since the 111 still had most of its speed. Whatever the pirate was flying—it looked like a Krager scout—it didn't have the juice to catch up and levelled out in pursuit half a klick back. Zham flew straight and level like a target sleeve, inviting the pirate to pour on the speed and line up his shot. Excitement buzzed in his veins, with the familiar edge of putting his life in someone else's hands.

"Now, Niko," he said.

"Here goes nothing."

The S-1 climbed slowly out of the Layer, trailing wild vortices of swirling lev from its wingtips. As Zham had hoped, the pirate was focused on their quarry and had entirely forgotten about their other opponent. An easy mistake to make in the heat of battle, but a costly one. Niko had a clear view of the underside of their aero, right from its blind spot.

She fired. The S-1 had only four guns, all in the wings, but the pirate's aero was thin-skinned. Bullets ripped along its underside from engine mount to the base of the tail. Gouts of flame immediately spewed from torn-open fuel tanks, momentarily turning the pirate into a fireworks display. Then it simply exploded, blooming into an ugly orange-and-black flower and spraying spinning pieces of aero across the sky.

"Holy *fuck*!" Niko shouted.

"Nice shooting." Zham turned back toward the convoy, head swiveling as he searched the sky. Niko swung in behind him.

"That guy's dead, right? Like definitely-definitely dead."

"Yeah." The one Zham had shot down might have time to bail out, if they could get past the spin. Pirates liked to bail under the Layer in any case, preferring to roll the dice on being retrieved by comrades rather than being picked up by their enemies and facing trial and execution.

"Okay! I totally killed a guy! I'm going to let that sink in for a bit. Niko Fanucci, a girl who kills people now."

"It's a hazard of the profession," Zham said.

"I'm aware of that. I'm just having a moment here."

There. Zham couldn't find the pirate who'd flown off, but he finally spotted the one Niko had winged, flying low to the Layer and still trailing a ribbon of black smoke. Zham swung toward him and thumbed back to Quedra's channel.

"Checking in," he said. "Two pirates down, one damaged, one fled. That's the lot."

"Nice flying," Quedra said after a moment's silence. "Aoife and Lanzo are getting warmed up. You can head back."

"I've got a better idea," Zham said, grinning. "Our friend here is leaking smoke pretty bad, and I don't think he knows I'm following. Ten to one he heads right back to base. Have Aoife load a couple of bombs and we can track down the mothership. There'll be a bounty in Aur Lunach for certain."

Another pause. Then, "No."

"What do you mean, *no*?" Zham said. "Gods know we need the money, and one less pirate crew in the world is always something to celebrate."

"I said no, Zham. It's too dangerous. Return to base."

"This is stupid." Other people were probably listening in ship-side, but Zham was past caring. "If we don't start taking a few chances, this company is going to go bust—"

"Don't argue with me while shells are flying, Zham. Return to base *now*."

Zham slapped the radio off and blistered the air in the cockpit with inventive profanity. But she was right—about that, at least. Discussion was for before and after a mission. He took a few breaths and clicked the set back on.

"Still there?" Niko said, on their private channel.

"More or less."

"Are we going back?"

Zham snorted. "You heard the orders."

"You're the flight leader," she said earnestly. "I take my orders from you."

For a few moments, Zham was tempted. If they brought down the pirate mothership, Quedra would scream her head off but they'd still get the bounty. Sev had told him to prove he was trustworthy; maybe that meant showing Quedra she wasn't always right, that Zham could make a good call.

But no, he decided regretfully. Aoife and Lanzo wouldn't take off without Quedra's approval, and it *was* too risky with just the two of them. If the pirates had any kind of anti-aero armament, or if they'd held any fliers in reserve, things could go badly wrong.

"I appreciate the vote of confidence," he said. "But we're done here."

* * *

"Woo!" Niko said, pushing back the cockpit as soon as the S-1 had come to a stop. "Okay. Okay! Still alive. Killed a guy. Feel like screaming. Woo!"

"Congratulations," Aoife said. She handed Niko a small glass of amber beer as she descended to the deck, then tapped it with her own. "Your first victories."

"Feels a bit like cheating," Niko said, downing her glass in a single swallow. "The first guy never saw me coming, and Zham set me up for the second one."

"Do this long enough," Zham said, climbing down from his own cockpit, "and you'll understand that the times they never see you coming are the best of all. Aoife, aren't you going up in a minute?"

"Aye," she said, looking sorrowfully at the beer, then handed it to him. "Congrats to you, too, I suppose."

"Woo!" said Niko for no apparent reason. "Sorry. Had one more of those to get out."

"Woo!" said Elli, emerging from the stairwell. Anni followed behind her. "Woo!"

"There is nothing like the excitement of combat," Lanzo said. "It reminds us we are still alive, you see?" He raised his eyebrows. "If you need release of stress, my young friend, I know many fine techniques."

"I can handle my own stress," Niko said, her own eyebrow quirked. "But right now, what I need is to sit down until I stop vibrating."

"And I—"

"Quedra wanted to talk to you," Aoife said.

"Yeah," Zham muttered. "That."

Quedra was on the bridge, as usual. Martin was absent, being off shift, so they were alone. There was a drone of engines from outside as Aoife prepped for takeoff. Quedra, seated at her table, waited until the noise faded before speaking.

"You ought to know better," she said.

"Better than what?" Zham said, his hackles already rising. "Than trying to make enough money to keep this operation flying?"

"Better than arguing a call during an engagement," she snapped. "Old Seegi would've had your hide."

Zham winced at the memory of his Academy sergeant, a man seemingly made entirely of boiled leather.

"Fine," he said. "That was wrong. But I was right about the pirates. Do you know how much we could have used even a small bounty? Sev has a list of repairs as long as—"

"What if they'd had another squadron waiting?"

Zham snorted. "If they'd had more aeros, they would have sent them. You don't live long as a pirate doing things by halves."

"And if not—"

"Then we'd fight them!"

"And maybe get shot up, and maybe die. You think we can afford to replace any aeros? Or any pilots?" She shook her head. "Getting the S-1 stretched our credit as it is."

"So, what's the plan, then? How are we going to turn things around?" Zham flopped into a chair opposite her. "Weren't we supposed to be building the best company south of the Cradle? We were going to show Na-yun and Li-Sal and all those fucking bastards—"

"*Zham.*"

Zham stopped and looked across the table at his sister. Really looked at her, for the first time in a while. There were more lines in her face than he remembered, and deep bags under her eyes. Those piercing eyes, always so full of fire, were . . . dulled.

"Come on," he said weakly. "You're the Diamond Knife, right? Hero of Gor-Bel-Sul? You can handle one ship and few sell-sticks."

"I used to think so," Quedra said, so quietly Zham wasn't sure he'd heard right. She sighed and brushed at her hair where it was escaping from its tail. "Just . . . don't go haring off on your own, all right? Not again."

A low blow, if not an unexpected one. Zham's face tightened. "Understood, *ma'am.*"

"You can stand a watch up here in penance," Quedra said, shoving her chair back from the table. She leaned heavily on her cane as she stood, and Zham had to force himself not to jump up to help. "Stomp on the floor if anything happens."

There was a small elevator in one corner, something Sev had improvised for Quedra's benefit. The room directly below the bridge, formerly the ship's map room, had been refitted as her cabin so she could make it up even on her bad days. Zham let out a breath as she closed the metal grate and sank out of sight with a squeal of metal.

A shift on the bridge was far from the worst punishment he'd ever been handed. In fact, it might be a blessing in disguise. The company's books, such as they were, were kept in a bulging filing cabinet; with a few hours alone, he might be able to get them in order. That would be making himself useful, right?

The paper football bounced off the wall, a few inches wide of the taped-up target, and Zham swore.

His resolve had lasted less than half an hour. The filing cabinet stood open, overflowing with receipts, scribbled notes, and a few logbooks that hadn't been updated in weeks. Quedra, for all her brilliance, despised paperwork almost as much as Zham did, and Martin rarely had the time or attention to attend to it. Zham's brief attempt to sort through it all had left him with a headache and a burning desire to do literally anything else, hence flicking wads of scrap paper at scribbled goalposts.

Aoife and Lanzo were still on station. With night rolling in, they'd be returning soon, and Martin would take over Zham's nominal duties. Not that he'd had to adjust course or even answer the radio.

As though the thought had been an invitation, there was a beep from the receiver. Zham shot to his feet, overturning his chair, and stumbled toward it. Sev had salvaged their set from a larger ship, rewiring only the parts they needed, so it had a great many more buttons and dials than strictly necessary. Zham searched the console until he found a blinking light and picked up the handset beside it. It screamed a rapidly shifting sequence of squealing tones in the nails-on-glass range into his ear and he slammed it down again.

The radioprinter began to chatter, paper winding out of its maw. He looked at it with suspicion. The things hadn't been accepted in the Navy before he'd left—and probably still weren't, the Protectorate being notoriously behind the times—but they'd become increasingly common in the Empire in the past decade. The block print on the curling strip of paper was certainly more legible than Zham's own scribbled shorthand.

Zham tore the strip off and skimmed it, picking out a few key phrases. *Offer of employment . . . the far south . . . fifty percent in advance . . .* And then a number, one that he had to carefully recheck in case his eager eyes had added an extra zero.

He blinked and looked around the bridge. Still empty.

There was supposed to be a carbon copy of all incoming communications, but no one had loaded the paper and the little bin was empty. The strip in Zham's hand was the only evidence.

If he brought it to Quedra, she'd take one look and throw it away. Not worth the risk. Not worth the time to even investigate.

So, obviously: don't bring it to Quedra.

The four of them sat in a corner of the empty mess, under a flickering bulb that made Zham feel like a conspirator in a kinema. The strip of paper sat on the table between them.

"I still don't like it," Aoife said.

"Which part?" Lanzo said. "The pile of money, or the fact that it's half up front?"

"Both, really," Aoife said. "It feels too good to be true."

Niko poked the paper where it specified the offered sum. "That's a lot, then?"

"It's a lot," Zham said. "Just the advance would be a huge help. Sev could take on parts in Aur Lunach and fix"—he waved a hand vaguely—"things. He has a list."

"And then we'd have to go into the wilds." Aoife glanced at Zham, then at Niko. "That means mantids. You've got . . ." She hesitated.

"I told Niko about Sam," Zham said.

"Ah." Aoife gave Niko a sympathetic smile. "Sorry. It didn't feel like my story to share."

"We can't stay out of the wilds for the rest of our lives," Zham said. "Not for this kind of money."

"*Definitely* not for this kind of money," Lanzo said. He was practically drooling.

"Quedra won't go for it, though," Aoife said. "You know that, Zham."

"She might, if we bring it to her the right way," Zham said. He leaned across the table. "That's where I need your help. Listen . . ."

CHAPTER
FOUR

Aur Lunach smelled of bugblood and industry.

The *Last Stop* had called at the city many times but rarely for long, and Zham wasn't as familiar with its streets—and pubs—as he was with Aur Marka's. Where the northern city was a hub for commerce across the Empire, Aur Lunach took advantage of its proximity to the wilds and specialized in mantid products, bugblood above all.

Mantids were *everywhere* along the docks, mostly in pieces. There were open boxes full of meter-long claws, stacks of legs sorted by size, stripped torsos like huge green cigars, and even a truck piled with a pyramid of heads like bright green cannonballs, their enormous compound eyes dulled in death. The only live specimens were mantid cows, bloated off-white creatures like wingless houseflies the size of a car, standing placidly in flimsy wooden containers stacked one atop the other. The big bugs were blind and deaf, responsive only to the pheromonal touch of their mantid handlers, and when dosed with the right scent, they would walk calmly into the slaughterhouse to have their bodily fluids drained.

Or so Niko informed Zham as they walked along. For his part, Zham had mostly stayed away from the sharp end of the mantid harvest. He knew, at an intellectual level, that the extract that fueled his aero ultimately came from the giant insects, but it was easier not to think about the crunchy, messy part of the process. Niko, however, looked on the dismembered bugs with fond familiarity.

"My family ran a bug trawler," she told Zham when he asked. "When I was six years old, I used to jump up and down on the shell-cracker to pry the bodies open. You ever had fresh mantid meat toasted over an open fire?" When Zham shook his head, Niko put on an expression of orgasmic bliss. "I don't miss the trawler, mostly, but those campfires . . ."

"There must be somewhere around here that serves fresh mantid," Zham said.

"Honestly, I'm scared to try it again. Probably won't live up to my expectations."

"Fair enough. So, what happened to the trawler?" Zham hesitated, thinking that through to the obvious tragic conclusion. "Oh, shit. Did—"

"No, nothing like that," Niko said, waving a hand. "Nobody got eaten or anything. I think Mom just got tired of smelling like bugblood all the time. We sold up and settled down in Aur Marka. Dad owns a butcher shop now."

"I guess carving up cows and pigs seems easy after three-meter insects."

"They're a lot less likely to rip your face off," Niko agreed. She eyed him sidelong. "Okay, now you owe me something—how'd you and your sister end up so far from the Protectorate?"

"Oof." Zham made a face. "That's a *long* story, and we're nearly there."

"Fine, but I'm calling in the marker next time we're on patrol."

"Anything except more I Spy." Zham pointed. "That's it, I think."

Their little expedition had required a bit of subterfuge. The job offer had come with an Aur Lunach telephone number; Aoife had lured Martin away from the bridge so Zham could use the ship-to-shore line. It had rung at a hotel, where a clerk had promised a callback; Lanzo had claimed to be expecting a ring from a ladyfriend and had thus intercepted the rendezvous time and place and passed it on to Zham. He'd claimed to be taking Niko out to show her the ropes of securing supplies, which had drawn skepticism from Quedra but not actual condemnation.

The address the hotel clerk had given them belonged to a restaurant called Talbot's, which even from the street started to make Zham feel underdressed. They pushed through the front door into a curtained anteroom, road noise vanishing behind them as though the rest of the world had ceased to exist. A waiter in formal black-and-white eyed them with barely concealed contempt.

Zham was wearing the best clothes he had, though he was well aware this hardly constituted fine dress. Under the waiter's eye, he bristled and wished he'd worn a filthy flight suit instead.

"Yes?" the man said, managing to pack so much venom into the syllable that it was a wonder his lips didn't sizzle.

"I'm Mr. Sa-Yool," he said, as the message had instructed. "We're expected."

The waiter consulted a small clipboard and his lip gave an unhappy quirk. "So it appears. Follow me, sir."

Discretion seemed to be Talbot's stock in trade. Every table had its own set of curtains that could be dropped to shield diners from prying eyes. There were no visible windows. Staff in formalwear moved about with the silent precision of undertakers.

"You ever been to a place like this?" Niko whispered, as they threaded their way through the maze-like rooms.

Zham shook his head and spoke a little too loud. "I wonder if the food is any good."

Their guide twitched but made no comment. Eventually, they arrived at a shrouded table and the waiter cleared his throat.

"Mr. Sa-Yool is here, sir. And a companion."

"*Mr.* Sa-Yool?" The voice had a heavy, nasal Academic accent. "Interesting. They are welcome, of course."

The waiter pulled the curtain aside, revealing a heavy, polished table in a small booth. A man and a woman sat on one side of it. Zham slid onto the bench opposite, Niko nervously pushing in beside him. When the curtain fell back, a wan light bulb in a velvet lampshade provided the only illumination.

"Greetings," the man said. He was pale and thin, with close-cropped dark hair, a long drooping mustache, and a monocle screwed tightly into his left eye. "I am Vyacheslav Nikolayevich Avilov, Professor Third Rank of the Loginov Academy. My companion is Xenia Ivanovna Oserova, Quadrivium of the same. I must admit to a little surprise, however. I was expecting Fleet Admiral Quedra Sa-Yool, and you do not resemble her."

"She no longer carries any Navy rank," Zham said, meeting the Academic's gaze and ignoring an incredulous look from Niko. "And if you're that well-informed, you've probably guessed that I'm her brother, Zham Sa-Yool."

"Ah, of course. Formerly Captain Sa-Yool of Gor-Bel-Sul fame."

"That was a long time ago," Zham said evenly. Inside, his guts were churning. It had been years since anyone had recognized them. "My companion is Nicolosa Fanucci, an aero pilot of *Last Stop*."

"Pleased to make your acquaintance, Ms. Fanucci." Avilov inclined his head. "And you have the authority to make agreements on your sister's behalf?"

"Of course," Zham lied blandly.

Avilov's lip twitched under his mustache. "I was looking forward to meeting the infamous Diamond Knife, but alas. Very well. Ms. Oserova, please explain the details?"

The woman cleared her throat. She was tall and solidly built, with square-rimmed eyeglasses, pale skin, and brown hair pulled into a severe bun and secured with long steel pins. Where Avilov wore a dark red robe with a white collar, she was dressed in an Imperial-style black pantsuit, creases sharp and tie impeccable. When she spoke, her accent was softer than her companion's.

"To understand the assignment, there is some amount of background," she said. "Twenty years ago or more, a certain professor—we will call him Victor—returned from a survey expedition in the wilds with claims of a discovery. A mountain valley at the upper edge of the green zone but surrounded on all sides by higher ground. Not as large as the Cradle, perhaps, but still substantial. You understand the value?"

Zham gave a slow nod. The green zone was everything below roughly a kilometer. At those low altitudes, the mantids and their symbiotically linked species thrived, and human habitation was impossible—the jungle rusted, eroded, wrecked, and eventually overgrew every barrier anyone had ever put in its way.

Above the green zone, the air thinned and dried, and the giant insects began to struggle. Humans could survive there, but it was always difficult to grow food and raise animals on high, rocky ground or terraces cut into mountainsides. Before the lev revolution, human life had always hovered on the edge, one bad harvest or mantid incursion away from disaster.

Except, that is, in the Cradle. A high, broad bowl nestled in the northern mountains, up beyond the green zone but with deep, rich soil and plentiful water, it was the only place yet discovered where humanity could truly prosper. Indeed, if the Anthropic priests Zham had grown up with were to be believed, it had been created specifically for mankind's use. It was the wealth of the Cradle that had made the Protectorate a world power. His own childhood had been spent in the border cities, outside the sacred boundaries, but his education had emphasized over and over that defending the Cradle was the primary purpose of the Protectorate and thus of the Navy at its sharp end.

In the rest of the world, not blessed with such perfect geography, the search for usable land never ended. In the last century, as lev-ships enabled longer voyages and made transport easier, the focus had been on ground that could be *defended*, even if it was below the line. Humans might not be able to build a city on the flats, but in a mountain valley with a narrow entrance, modern technology and firepower could hold the bugs off indefinitely. Such was the theory, in any case, although history was littered with over-mighty cities and nations who'd pushed their luck too far and been overwhelmed. Golden Szacus, heart of the once-united Empire, was only the latest example.

Still, new attempts were always ongoing. For ambitious people, the discovery of a new hidden valley was an opportunity to expand their power; for merchant speculators, it was a chance to gamble fortunes for spectacular profits. The newspapers and explorer's taverns were always full of hints and rumors. The location of a hitherto-unknown spot was information of inestimable value.

Zham wasn't sure if Niko was following, but he kept his eyes on Xenia. "Was Victor's discovery confirmed?"

"Victor played his cards close to the chest, as the Imperials say," she said, sounding pleased he understood the import. "He was a powerful man and a wealthy one. He and a few other backers funded a colonizing expedition, and he led it himself. They disappeared into the south without telling anyone precisely where they were going. But for a few years, at least, they must have thrived. Supply ships came and went with tight-lipped crews. And then . . . nothing." She spread her hands. "No more ships, and no radio contact."

"Sounds like it wasn't perfect after all," Niko said, somewhat to Zham's surprise.

"That was the assumption in the Academies," Avilov said. "That Victor's claims, which had never been backed with evidence, did not pan out and that he and his expeditions eventually perished. However, in a search of records here in Aur Lunach, I discovered the diary of a freighter captain who visited the colony. Though enjoined to secrecy, he sketched what had been done, the lay of the ground, and more importantly recorded the exact location. *If* his report is to be believed, the valley is everything Victor claimed."

"Then what happened to Victor?" Zham said.

"That is what you are going to find out," Avilov said. "I do not have Victor's funding, nor his hubris, to try and exploit this on my own. But the man who brings such a discovery to his Academy will gain great wealth and prestige. Unless it does not pan out, in which case he would merely look like a fool. I do not enjoy looking like a fool.

"Therefore, your company will undertake a journey to Victor's lost colony and attempt to discover what happened and whether it truly is as it appears. Ms. Oserova will accompany you and retain custody of the precise location until it is needed. On your return, you will be bound not to speak of what you have seen until I have established academic priority—a matter of weeks. Then you will be free to go on your way with the second half of the payment. Are these acceptable terms?"

Zham looked between them, mouth suddenly dry. "May I ask a question?"

"Of course," Xenia said. Avilov looked sour.

"Your message was coded specifically for the *Last Stop*. Why us?"

Avilov gave a quiet chuckle. "I have always been an . . . admirer, shall we say, of your sister. Even in the Academies, we have heard of the Diamond Knife and her victories. When I learned that she was leading a mercenary company, it seemed a poetic twist of fate. And though I only know her by reputation, that reputation is clear with regard to her sense of duty. I believe I can trust her—and, by extension, her crew—not to attempt to circumvent our arrangement."

That certainly *would* be a concern, Zham was sure. On the way back, if all went well, the *Last Stop* would be in possession of an incredibly valuable secret. The temptation to throw Xenia over the side and sell it to the highest bidder would be considerable. But

Avilov had the right of it—Quedra's sense of honor, battered and bruised as it had become, would never allow such a thing.

Zham was well aware of what he *ought* to do, which was make a polite exit, return to the ship, and somehow find a way to break the whole thing to Quedra. With all the information, he might be able to make her see reason. The job was *perfect*—the high pay was the premium for keeping a secret, a task for which she was admirably suited and which entailed no additional danger. If everything went well, it might even bring them some level of fame—more work, a better class of employer—

And she would torpedo the whole thing if he let her. Absolutely, unquestionably. Because it was outside the groove she'd decided was safe, she'd find some excuse. She would—

"We'll do it," Zham said, before he'd fully realized he'd made the decision. He slapped one hand on the table. "We accept the job."

Niko elbowed him in the ribs, and he glanced over to see her eyes wide. He shook his head briefly.

"Excellent," Avilov said, as though he'd expected no other result. "Ms. Oserova will present herself at your ship tomorrow morning. I trust you can leave soon?"

"We'll need a few days to load fresh supplies," Zham said. "But soon enough."

"Very good." Avilov brushed off the front of his robe. "Then I believe our business is concluded. I bid you good day."

"Um." Niko put up a hesitant hand. "Do they actually have *food* at this restaurant?"

They did, as it turned out, but the prices were beyond the reach of ordinary mortals, and the Academics made no offer to pay. Niko was still bitter about that, muttering dangerously to herself.

"He's hiring the whole damn ship. Wouldn't kill him to spring for a steak. Nice and rare, with butter and a little pepper . . ."

Zham was only half-listening. He was thinking about how to spin the job to Quedra, whether there would be enough cash left to buy some replacement parts for the 111 he'd had his eye on, and—though he was reluctant to admit it to himself—the way Ms. Oserova had given him a tight smile when they'd shaken hands. She had a firm grip, and the severe lines of her suit couldn't *entirely* conceal—

"Zham!"

"What?" He tried to replay the last few seconds of monologue. "Do you want me to buy you a steak? We can find somewhere a little more reasonable."

"No! Actually, yes, absolutely, let's please do that, but it's not what I was asking. Are you sure you know what you're doing with this?"

"Absolutely," Zham lied.

"You've got a plan to explain this to your sister?"

"I've been dealing with Quedra for a long time." Though, if pressed, he would have had to admit that never during that expanse of years had he succeeded in talking her into doing something she'd set herself against. *Stubborn* didn't begin to cover it. "It's all about how you lead in to the subject. You've got to slip it in subtly so she doesn't dig her heels in right at the outset. Let her convince herself it's a good idea."

"Sounds tricky," Niko said, "but you're the expert."

That was going a bit far, but Zham accepted it with a regal nod. "You'll see."

"Now, about that—"

"Hello, my friends!"

The new voice had a clipped, sharp tone that Zham associated with Imperial authority. It emerged from a man who'd stepped directly in front of them, his hand presented to Zham. He wore a gray jacket of a military cut over a ruffled shirt, and his creased trousers bore a single red stripe. Intelligent blue eyes looked out from under a peaked cap and above a pencil-thin mustache waxed into points.

Zham looked down at the hand and, for lack of anything else to do, took it. His interlocutor shook exactly twice, as precisely as some circus automaton.

"I would like to buy you a drink," the man said.

"Thanks," Zham said. "But we're a little busy."

He moved to circle around, but the man sidestepped neatly in front of him, still smiling.

"I must *insist* on buying you a drink," he said. "And perhaps in the course of such an encounter, we might discuss some business that would be of mutual benefit."

Zham looked around in case there were a dozen thugs waiting in an alley. But the man appeared to be alone.

"I'm not aware of having business with anyone in Aur Lunach," he said. "If you'll excuse us—"

The man's smile broadened. Two of his teeth were bright and golden.

"I must," he repeated with a hint of menace, "*insist.*"

There was a pause.

"Forget drinks," Niko said. "Buy me a steak and you can talk all you want."

The man's head snapped round and he beamed.

"A steak can be arranged as well! Please follow me."

Then there was nothing for it but to go with him. It was Zham's turn to give Niko a look, to which she responded with a big-eyed *Who, me?* expression. The stranger led them to a restaurant of a more ordinary sort, with bustling clientele and red-checked tablecloths. Niko collared a waiter immediately and demanded her cherished steak, while Zham, with a shrug, asked for sausage, potato, and beer. The stranger took only a glass of red wine.

"You are Zham Sa-Yool," the man said, which brought up the old punch-in-the-face-and-run instinct in Zham. "I do not know your young companion, I'm afraid."

"Niko," Niko said, her mouth full of meat.

"I am Erich Aur-Brahda, at your service." He inclined his head.

Zham's eyebrows rose a fraction. That explained the accent, at least—the "aur" part of the name marked Erich as coming from the old Imperial nobility. A rare distinction nowadays, as most of the ancient lines had vanished in the destruction of Szacus and the chaos that followed.

"Nice to make your acquaintance," Zham said cautiously. "If I may ask, what do you want with us?"

"I wanted to ask you about your conversation with a pair of Academics earlier today," Erich said. "I understand it was in connection to hiring your ship, the *Last Stop*. Or, rather, the ship captained by your sister Quedra."

Zham had grown used to being anonymous in the last decade, and he was getting annoyed at everyone seeming to know his business. "Our discussions with clients are private," he snapped.

"Of course they are. You will carefully not tell me that you discussed an expedition to a certain valley, where a certain Academic's lost colony is thought to reside."

"I don't know what you're talking about."

"Indeed! Nor will you when I inquire whether your new partners saw fit to divulge to you the colony's precise location."

"Even if they had," Zham said through gritted teeth, "I wouldn't tell you."

"In the event that such information *were* available to you," Erich said, pulling a pen from his breast pocket and scribbling on his napkin, "this is what I would be prepared to pay for it."

Zham couldn't help glancing down, just for a moment. Once again he had to count zeroes. It was more than Avilov's entire promised payment, probably enough to buy the *Last Stop* outright. He raised his beer to wet his suddenly dry lips.

"As I said. I don't know what you're talking about."

There was a long silence, broken only by the sound of Niko's furious mastication. Erich was no longer smiling.

"Very well," he said, with frosty politeness. "May I offer some advice, at least?"

"I'm not sure I can stop you," Zham said.

"Stay away from any job those Academics offer. Their proposal is more dangerous than it appears." He got to his feet and leaned across the table, all traces of humor gone, gold teeth gleaming. "I guarantee it."

Erich snapped back to military straightness, gave them both a nod, and left, dropping coins in the hands of the surprised waiter as he went. Niko scarfed the last of her steak, swallowing too fast and thumping her chest in agitation until Zham handed her a glass of water.

"You ate that whole thing *already*?" he said. He'd barely touched his plate.

"I thought we were going to have to run for it again!" Niko said, clutching her empty plate protectively. "No beef left behind."

Zham laughed out loud, and after a moment, Niko joined him. He leaned back in his chair, and she eyed him, then looked to his plate.

"Are you going to eat that sausage?"

"Help yourself."

"Mmrf," she said moments later, mouth full. "Surprised you didn't take that guy's offer seriously. The money's the important thing, right?"

"Only if we actually get it," Zham said. "The Academics didn't give us the location, and I doubt he'd pay up without checking."

"So, are we still doing the job? He sounded serious."

A slow smile spread across Zham's face. "Oh, now we're *definitely* doing the job."

"Just have to figure out how to convince Quedra." Niko bolted the end of the sausage. "You've got a plan, right?"

"Of course," Zham said. "Nothing to worry about."

CHAPTER FIVE

"Zham!"

Someone was shaking him. Zham rolled over, as much as the little bunk allowed, and groaned.

"Zham, get *up*!"

"Wha's goin' on?" he mumbled. "Ship on fire?"

"Not yet, but Quedra's getting there," Niko said. "That Academic woman is here *now*. I thought you had a plan!"

"I do," Zham said. "Jus' need to wait till morning, talk to . . . talk to Quedra . . ."

Slowly, his brain jolted into full operation, coughing and sputtering like a recalcitrant aero. When it caught, he sat bolt upright, forcing Niko to jump backward.

"What time is it?"

"Past nine," Niko said.

"Oh, fuck," Zham said. "And Xenia's *here*?"

"She turned up on the dock and Quedra let her on board! When I left, they were just kind of staring at each other."

"Oh, *fuck*," Zham said. "Why didn't you wake me up?"

"I *did* wake you up!"

He wasn't listening anymore, rapidly throwing on a bare minimum of clothes and fumbling with the laces of his boots. This turn of events was, to put it lightly, really gods-damned bad—if the way to convince Quedra was to work her around to something gradually, the *worst* thing to do was to surprise her. The Diamond Knife hated surprises.

Niko was hard-pressed to keep up as Zham ran through the bowels of the *Last Stop*, boots clanging on metal floors as he vaulted rails and took the steps three at a time. By the time he reached the landing outside the bridge, most of the rest of the crew were gathered there already. Aoife, Lanzo, and Karl gave Zham the sad-eyed looks directed at a funeral's guest of honor, while Anni and Elli were less circumspect.

"She's gonna tear you a new one," Elli said.

"A new one!" Anni said, then added, "A new what?"

"Never mind," Karl said, putting a hand on their shoulders. He jerked his head at the door. "You'd better go in. They're waiting."

"A new butthole, *actually*," Elli said behind her father's back.

Zham opened the door.

Quedra was in her wheelchair, which meant it was a bad day. The expression on her face was frostily polite. Xenia sat across from her, still in her sharp suit, a black leather bag held primly on her knees like a shield. The Academic was hard to read behind her glasses, but the look she shot at Zham was annoyed.

Martin, waiting silently to one side, closed the door to block out the crowd of eavesdroppers. Quedra looked up at Zham over steepled hands.

"Good morning, brother," she said—the "brother" was a *bad* sign; if she felt the need to remind everyone of their familial relationship, things were already at a low point—"Good of you to join us. I've been having the most fascinating conversation with Ms. Oserova."

"I, um, apologize for oversleeping," Zham said. "Quedra, if I could just talk to you alone for a moment—"

"She tells me," Quedra went on relentlessly, "that yesterday you had a meeting with her and her superior and came to an agreement regarding some work. Somehow, she was under the impression that you had the authority to agree to a contract on behalf of our company."

"He told us as much," Xenia said severely. The look she gave him was now *definitely* annoyed, heading rapidly toward pissed off.

Zham squirmed. "I may have *slightly* stretched the facts there. But if I could just have a minute alone with my sister, I'm certain we can clear this up—"

"You don't think Ms. Oserova would be interested?" Quedra said, letting the moment stretch on while Zham shifted uncomfortably. Finally, she sighed. "Very well. Martin, could you take our guest to the mess and offer her some refreshment?"

"Of course, ma'am," Martin said.

Zham waited another few excruciating seconds in silence as Xenia rose, gave him another frown, and followed Martin out. He got a brief glimpse of everyone outside watching to see if Quedra had flayed him alive, but the door quickly shut again.

"First of all," Zham said, "let me say that this was not how I hoped this would play out—"

"Doubtless," Quedra said dryly. "*Please* tell me this isn't just you trying to get this woman into bed."

"No!" Zham said, indignant to cover a hint of guilt. "This is about saving the company. This is about you. You and me, I mean. Us."

"Us." Her eyes were hooded. "You want to elaborate?"

"I was talking with Sev. Complaining, really." Zham flopped into the chair Xenia had vacated, shoulders slumping. "I know things are going badly and I want to *help*. But when I told Sev that you won't let me, they asked whether I'd done anything to make you feel like you can trust me."

"Sev can be perceptive," Quedra said.

It stung Zham to hear it but he pressed onward regardless. "That stuck with me. I kept thinking about it."

"Really." She sat up a little. "Is that why you wanted to go after those pirates so badly?"

"Something like that." Zham shrugged. "When this job came in, I thought it looked perfect. I figured I'd take care of getting it set up, show you how great everything looked, and . . . maybe you'd be willing to trust my judgment." Fat chance of that happening *now*. Zham's gut twisted.

Quedra raised an eyebrow. "What happened?"

"I . . . uh . . ." He sank even lower in the chair. "Overslept."

She stared at him for a second, eyes hooded, expression blank. Then the corner of her mouth twitched, she gave a snort, and finally she laughed, cradling her face in her hands. Zham froze, face growing redder by the moment. He'd expected her to shout, but *this*—

"I'll go tell Xenia the deal's off," he muttered, pushing his chair back.

"Wait." Quedra held up a hand, gasping for breath. "Wait. I'm sorry, really. It's just so . . . so *Zham*."

"Excuse me for living," Zham snapped.

"I do, gods help me." Quedra wiped her eyes and leaned back. "Okay. Ms. Oserova gave me the gist. Is there anything you want to add?"

"To add—" he parroted, then sat up straighter. "You want to do it?"

"Well, you've put the honor of the *Last Stop* at stake, haven't you?" she drawled. "So, I'm thinking about it. Why should we?"

"You've seen the fee?"

"It's certainly attractive."

"Half up front, too. Sev and Karl both have parts lists as long as my arm. We can load up and spend the trip south doing repairs."

"You don't think it's too good to be true?"

"I worried about that," Zham said. "But a big part of the deal is us keeping quiet, and they're willing to pay extra for that. Avilov trusts you."

"*Me?* Why?"

"He's . . . a fan, I guess you'd say? Of the Diamond Knife."

"Really." Quedra's eyebrows went up. "I didn't think anybody knew that name south of Polrock."

"The Academics know everything, I guess," Zham said. "And since Xenia—Ms. Oserova, I mean—is coming with us, we know they're not going to try leave us in the lurch."

"You want to use her as a hostage?" Quedra sounded surprised.

"Not *literally*," Zham said. "It just seems good to have a little—collateral, say."

"We wouldn't exactly be able to go to law with them in Imperial court, I imagine," Quedra murmured. "All right."

"*All right* meaning—"

"Meaning one more question."

She rocked her wheelchair back and around the table. Her legs were wrapped in a blanket, which usually meant a *really* bad day. She'd described her pain often enough that Zham could imagine what she was feeling, but her face didn't show it. Instead, she seemed full of concern, and she put a hand on his arm.

"You know what this would mean, right?" she said. "If we do this."

"A decent payday for once?" Zham said, though he could guess what she meant.

"A trip into the wilds means mantids."

"Mantids are always a possibility."

"This would make it a certainty," she said. "You haven't flown against bugs since . . . then."

"Since Sam died." *Tell Zham that I wish he'd asked me out some-time.* He wished his throat didn't feel tight. "I know."

"Are you sure you're ready?"

"We all cared about Sam," Zham said, speaking slowly to make sure his voice didn't betray him. "She was . . ."

"I know."

"But people die. It's a hazard of the job."

"I know."

"I'll be all right."

He suspected she knew how hard he was struggling to keep his composure, and he felt absurdly grateful when she patted his arm and wheeled backward. If there were tears glittering in her own eyes, she quickly hid them behind the diamond mask.

"In that case," she said, all business, "as captain of the *Last Stop*, I officially approve of your negotiations on our behalf. Please apologize to Ms. Oserova for the confusion and get her situated." She made a face. "When you pick a room for her, make sure it gets cleaned before she sees it."

"Of course, Captain." Zham bounced to his feet, swallowing the lump in his throat and breaking into a grin.

"And, Zham?" Quedra said, before he could leave.

"Yes?"

"I want you on the straight and narrow until this is over. Is that understood?"

He drew himself up and gave her a real Navy salute, muscle memory still strong after a decade. "Aye, Captain!"

A cup of hot tea and half an hour cooling her heels had evidently not mollified Xenia, and she kept her skeptical look all through Zham's explanation and apology. When he was finished, she got up, brushing dust from her trousers, and gave him a haughty look.

"Well," she said. "It appears we will be working together after all, then."

"It appears we will," Zham said. "I'm glad we will, I mean."

"My bags are waiting in the hangar," she said. "If your crew can assist me getting them stowed?"

It was a command, not a request. Zham looked toward the doorway and saw three small heads poking around it. Niko, Elli, and

Anni giggled and vanished, but Niko returned when Zham cleared his throat.

"Hi," she said, waving at Xenia. "Sorry. We were, um, sorry."

"There are children on board?" Xenia said.

"Yes?" Zham said, drawing the word out in embarrassment.

"Are they yours?"

"Wh—what?" If he'd had a drink in hand, it would have been a magnificent spit take; as it was, he merely stuttered stupidly. "No, of course not! They belong to Karl, our aircraft mechanic."

"We don't *belong* to anyone, *actually*," Elli said from behind the doorframe.

"Yes, thank you for that," Zham said. "Go and tell your dad we need help with Ms. Oserova's luggage. Where's Aoife?"

"Downstairs, getting the room ready," Niko said. "She should be nearly done."

"All right!" Zham clapped his hands. "Ms. Oserova, welcome to the *Last Stop*."

Xenia sniffed. Her eyebrows rose a little with every patch of flaking paint and rusty fixture they passed, and went up the rest of the way when they reached the hangar deck, half-crammed with scrap and loose parts. Karl was waiting with a dour expression beside a pile of leather-bound traveling trunks considerably larger than Xenia herself.

"You don't travel light, do you?" Niko said.

"We are venturing into the wilds," Xenia said, with only a trace of defensiveness. "One must be prepared for all contingencies."

"Prob'ly gonna cost us half the fee in extra fuel," Karl said, though given the state of the hangar, Zham thought that was patently unfair. "I sent the girls to get some more help."

"And help has arrived!" Lanzo said, appearing in the doorway. He gave Xenia an extravagant bow and offered his hand. "I understand my lady needs some assistance?"

Xenia looked at him like he'd crawled out from under a rock, then gestured at the pile of trunks. "Get started, then."

"Gladly," Lanzo said with a smooth smile. He sized up the stack, grabbed the largest trunk, and heaved it on his shoulder. Or tried to; in any event, he only got it as far as his chest. Smile straining, he staggered toward the door.

Ingeborg, coming in behind him, gave Zham a silent nod and hoisted a large bag in each hand, edging around Lanzo. Zham himself carried a smaller bag as he escorted Xenia down two flights to the crew deck.

Aoife was waiting by one of the larger cabins, hastily emptied of extra stores and provided with clean linen. Even so, Zham thought that Xenia's bags would practically fill the place. The Academic gave the surroundings a grim look, as though her worst expectations had been confirmed.

"It will suffice," she said. "Now I would like some privacy, please. I have a report to compose."

Aoife raised a hand in greeting, but Xenia closed the door in both of their faces.

"Seems like a lovely girl," Aoife said. "Charming."

"Charming," Zham muttered.

Fortunately, he did not have to see very much of their passenger over the next couple of days. Sev made a rare appearance, leaving their warren for the first time in ages to venture into the city, and Zham was recruited for an escort-slash-pack mule. The old engineer had a shopping list and an itinerary that seemed to cover half the warehouses, junk shops, and scrapyards in Aur Lunach; parts too heavy to go into Zham's rapidly filling backpack were delivered to the docks, where Ingeborg and a perspiring Lanzo were put to work hauling them. Dock stevedores used cranes to load the heavier pieces, along with the crates of fresh perishables and other supplies. Huge hoses were mated to their sockets on the sides of the ship, pumping in fresh water, liquid lev, and bugblood in a variety of grades.

It would take more than a quick infusion of cash to make the *Last Stop* as good as new—a year in drydock might not be enough—but when the ship finally lifted up and away from Aur Lunach, she was at least better off than she'd been in some time. Karl puttered away happily on the aeros, replacing hoses and filters long past their expiration dates, while down in the depths of the engine deck, Sev banged away on his mysterious machinery. Quedra agreed to run at half-power for the first leg of the journey, down to the refueling stop at Theovan, so that the engineer could shut down one engine at a time for maintenance.

Out for a stroll on the flight deck once they were properly underway, Zham spotted a tall figure near the bow. As he ambled over, he saw that it was Xenia, arms spread wide as though ready to wrap someone in a bear hug. She'd taken off her jacket, carefully folding it under her black bag lest it blow away, and let her hair loose from its bun. There was enough wind over the bow to stream it behind her and make her trouser legs flap wildly, but she didn't seem to mind.

Zham found himself smiling with nostalgia. The sky overhead was a brilliant azure blue, the sun bright but without much heat. The Layer was unbroken ahead, a sea of blue-white cloud in a slow-motion roil. Ships' crews became jaded to the beauty of the clear air and sunshine, but for a groundling it could be transformative.

"Is this your first time above the Layer?" he said.

Xenia gave a gasp and spun around, her cheeks coloring as though he'd caught her doing something untoward. She fumbled her spectacles out of her breast pocket and snapped them open, and only once she had them on did she relax slightly.

"Oh. Mr. Sa-Yool."

"Sorry," Zham said. "I didn't mean to scare you."

"Without these"—she tapped her glasses—"everything past a meter is a blur."

"I can see how that would make you jumpy."

She smiled slightly, then seemed to grow self-conscious about this admission of vulnerability and drew herself up again, one hand automatically gathering her hair.

"So, is it?" Zham said. "Your first time, I mean."

"No, strictly speaking," she said. "I came to Aur Lunach from Riskanej on a passenger liner. But my cabin did not have a view, and I spent the time studying my assignment."

"Everyone should get up here from time to time." Zham shaded his eyes with his hand as he stared up into the blue. "Makes me feel alive."

"It's certainly . . . refreshing." Xenia's face was still ruddy from the wind. "You misled us, back at our meeting. Why?"

Zham let out a breath. "It's complicated. My sister and I . . . sometimes don't see eye to eye."

"It must be difficult, standing in her shadow."

Zham snorted. "*That* isn't the difficult part." He hesitated a moment. "How much do you know about her?"

"Professor Avilov briefed me on her career. The great victory at Gor-Bel-Sul."

"He didn't mention how we ended up here?"

"No." She pursed her lips. "I admit I was curious about that."

"I imagine there's an official version in the Navy archives," Zham said. "But the real story goes like this. After Gor-Bel-Sul, the northern rebels were on the back foot, reduced to defending their main fortress at Gartop. Quedra was assigned to find a way to winkle them out. She decided to—well, the details aren't important. It was a good plan, bold and imaginative, exactly the sort of thing you'd expect from the Diamond Knife."

"What happened?"

"Disaster." Zham closed his eyes, remembering. Screams on the radio and fire overhead. The sky thick with the smoke of burning ships. "The worst defeat since the Fenkin War." That particular defeat, he abruptly recalled, had been at the hands of *her* people. He moved on quickly. "The Navy blamed Quedra. Said she'd gotten overconfident, believed she could do no wrong."

"You don't agree?"

He scratched the back of his neck. "I'm no master tactician, but I know my sister. She spends every waking moment imagining what could go wrong. And the plan *was* good. It just . . . went wrong." He sighed. "In any event, she was offered the traditional choice between exile and falling on her sword. I think they expected her to take the *honorable* way out, but once again, it shows they don't know Quedra like I do. She will never, ever give up."

"You admire her," Xenia said, smiling slightly.

"Yeah," Zham said uncomfortably. "She's been through a lot."

"What about you?"

"Me? I have it easy."

Xenia chuckled. "No, I mean, were you punished as well?"

"Oh, no. I wasn't senior enough to make a good scapegoat." He gave an embarrassed shrug. "I, uh, got a commendation, actually. But when they told me Quedra was being thrown out of the Navy, I gave the brass the finger and went with her."

"That was a brave thing to do."

"I guess. It was, um, spur of the moment."

"I can imagine."

"If we're being honest," Zham said, "I wouldn't know what to do with myself without her giving me orders."

Xenia burst into laughter, covering her mouth with one hand. Zham, reddening, tried to change the subject.

"What about you?" he said. "Have you always been"—he realized he didn't actually know *what* her job really was—"uh, assisting Avilov? Or . . . what?"

"He chose me to be his Primary Adjunct a year and a half ago," she said, chest swelling. "It's a great honor."

"And is this the sort of thing you usually do for him? Sail off into the wilds?"

She laughed again. "Oh, no. This is my first time doing any kind of fieldwork." Now it was her turn to look embarrassed. "I'm not sure I really have any relevant skills. My primary focus is forensic accounting, you see. Digging through old ledgers to find irregularities, that sort of thing. The only reason I'm here is because the professor trusts me, and this assignment is obviously . . . sensitive."

"Well," Zham said gallantly, "you shouldn't need to do more than take in the view. We've got this under control."

"I certainly hope so, Mr. Sa-Yool."

"Oof." He gave a sheepish grin. "Please call me Zham. We don't stand on ceremony around here."

She looked taken aback for a moment, then gave a cautious smile in return. "You may call me Xenia, if you like. As Untutored"—she hesitated, then corrected herself—"as non-Academics, that is, you are not required to use any formal address."

"Xenia, then."

There was a moment of embarrassed silence.

"I should go," she said, turning away. "The professor sent me with a good deal of work to occupy my time, and he expects regular updates. Thank you for the insight into your sister. I hope to get to know her better." She paused awkwardly. "And you as well, of course."

"Likewise," Zham said. He gave her a little wave as she walked up the deck.

"Youuuuuu fancy her," came a voice from behind a pumping station.

"What?" Zham turned and saw a red-headed face among the pipes. "Good gods, Niko, what are you doing here?"

"Having a very nice nap in the sun," she said, stretching, "until *somebody* interrupted me. But in return, I got some juicy gossip."

"How much of that did you hear?"

"Most of it. Enough to get the gist." She leaned over the pipe. "Did you know the back of your neck turns red when you blush?"

"Niko! You might have said something."

"And ruin the moment?"

Zham sighed. "What moment?"

"Oh, come *on*. You were practically drooling."

"I'll grant that she's . . . reasonably attractive"—considerably more than that; the hints of curves under the sharp lines of that suit were doing strange things to Zham's anatomy—"but you heard her talk. It sounds like she's half in love with Professor Avilov as it is. And I didn't get the impression that her opinion of *me* is very high."

"Mmmm, I wouldn't be so certain," Niko said, putting a finger to her lips.

"Says you, with your vast experience in the ways of love."

"I have watched *Whisper My Name* at the kinema seventy-nine times, I'll have you know," she said. "And read every volume of *Fen & Vicki*, even the silly one where Vicki loses her memory and thinks she's the Szacine Empress and only Fen's kiss can bring her back."

"Well, in that case, I withdraw my objection," Zham said. "But just so you know, next time we have shore leave, you and I are going on an *adventure*."

"You corruptor of innocent youth," Niko said with a grin.

Zham's own smile faded. "You heard the rest, then?"

"About Quedra? Yeah." Niko shifted uncomfortably. "Sorry."

"*That* you're sorry about eavesdropping on?"

"Seems different," Niko said. "I won't tell anyone."

Zham shrugged. "It's not really a secret. Everyone in the crew has heard the story. It's just—"

"Not something we talk about," Niko said. "I get it."

"At least not where she might hear it," Zham said.

Niko nodded. "For what it's worth," she said, "I think Xenia's right."

"What about?"

"It was a brave thing to do, going into exile with her."

"At the time," Zham said, with another shrug, "it felt like the easy way out."

CHAPTER
SIX

Days passed. There was little traffic there, out beyond all but the most tenuous boundaries of the Empire, so Quedra kept the patrols on deck to save fuel, and they stood watches with binoculars on the bridge instead. It was a relief at first—Niko could find things to amuse herself apart from playing I Spy—but after a few shifts, Zham found himself itching to fly.

From above the Layer, the wilds never seemed very wild, apart from the odd storm. Down below, Zham knew, the lowlands rolled on and on, unbroken by any heights poking beyond the green zone and thus entirely unfit for human habitation. On the far southern edge of this basin of toxic green were a few scattered peaks, the forerunners of a more rumpled landscape. One of these hosted Theovan, the final outpost of civilization, providing fuel and food to the hunters and prospectors who ventured beyond.

The ship shuddered and groaned as it sank through the Layer, catching the chaotic winds that churned the lev-clouds. When they emerged, the world beneath seemed dim and gray by comparison with the bright skies above. The ground was a uniform carpet of sickly green jungle. A lone mountain stood out from the plain like a cat under a bedsheet, a single spire breaking free of the clinging trees to rise high enough to become a spike of bare rock.

Theovan clung to the sheer side of the mountain, a scrotal bulge beneath the phallic peak. The station was a large, incomplete disc, like a thick slice of cucumber with a wedge removed, that open angle being where it was attached to the rock by a complicated set of steel spurs. More beams reached out to brace it from underneath, giving it the look of being caught in a spider's web.

Docks protruded from the outside of the circle, and to everyone's surprise, one of them was occupied. As the *Last Stop* eased into its final approach under Martin's capable handling, the rest of the crew gathered on the flight deck to gawk.

"That," Aoife said, speaking the general sentiment aloud, "looks expensive."

The other ship was half again as long as the *Last Stop* but no wider, with a tapered hull giving her the sleek look of a flattened cigar. A raked-back conning tower rose amidships, and she sported squat turrets fore and aft, each mounting what looked to Zham like 10 cm guns. Several blisters along either side were probably machine-gun pods.

"She's not a pure gunship, or she'd carry a lot more firepower," Lanzo said. "Somebody's private yacht?"

Karl shook his head, his jealousy almost palpable. "There's hangar doors for loading at the bottom, see? It's a trailhook carrier. No flight deck, just drop the aeros like bombs to launch and pick them up with a line and hook. The latest thing."

"Not sure I'd be comfortable being hurled off the ship like yesterday's lunch," Niko said.

"Not sure *I'd* be comfortable without somewhere to land," Zham said.

"Only works if you have auxiliary lev tanks on the aeros, obviously," Karl said, annoyed that not everyone was drooling over the stranger like he was. "Trailhook is the future. Another couple of decades and we'll all be using it."

"Where's she from?"

"Has to be an Anark, right?" Lanzo said. "Looking like that."

"GRE-001," Xenia said. Everyone looked round. She held a pair of advanced-looking binoculars in both hands, peering at the markings that mottled the sleek ship's hull. "Out of Newer Liberty, looks like."

"Can you see the name?" Zham said.

She refocused on the stern and frowned. "*Move Fast & Break Things*, it says."

Lanzo snorted. "*Definitely* Anarks."

Xenia lowered the binoculars. "I'll have to make a report to the professor." She looked at Zham. "Do you think they're going to be a problem?"

"I can't see why they would be," Zham said slowly. But the back of his neck was prickling. He couldn't think of any reason why a brand-new Anark cruiser would be out there either.

His premonition proved to be correct. When *Last Stop* had settled in beside the *Move Fast*, Quedra's call to the station asking for fueling was met with the curt response that the fueling pumps were occupied. Irritated, Quedra asked Zham to sort it out, and so he found himself clanging across the corrugated metal docks with Niko, who'd volunteered as assistant.

"If you're hoping for a good time," Zham warned her, "you're going to be disappointed. These long-range outposts are usually pretty grim."

"Beats rattling around the mess," Niko said. "Maybe we'll see some Anarks. You ever meet an Anark?"

"A few times."

"What are they like?"

Zham shrugged. "Just people."

"I heard they'd all sell their own mothers for an extra couple of marks."

"You're saying most Imperials wouldn't?"

Niko cocked her head, considering. "Doubt I could get more than a mark fifty for mine."

A hatch led into the interior of the station, and stenciled signs led Zham along brown-painted corridors to the stationmaster's post. The door was open; Zham knocked on the wall for politeness and went in.

Like *Last Stop*'s bridge, this was a spot designed to get a panoramic view, raised like a glassed-in bubble on the flat top of the station. What that actually amounted to was a wide-ranging look at nothing in particular; there were just the Layer above and the jungle far below stretching out to the hazy horizon. The tops of the two docked ships were visible as well, along with the forest of antennas that festooned the station's roof.

A row of communication equipment even more opaquely complex than the set aboard the *Last Stop* occupied one wall, staffed by a bored-looking young woman in an Aur Lunach military uniform. Another man oversaw a set of blinking lights and dials of no obvious purpose. In the center of the room was a large swiveling chair, and there sat the stationmaster, a heavily built, balding man in late middle age who dabbed his brow with a handkerchief that was already half-sodden. He turned to face Zham, calling over his shoulder.

"Stanley!"

"Sir?" the blinking-lights-man said.

"Who are these people?"

"I think they're from the *Last Stop*, sir."

"That's right," Zham said, shoving his verbal foot in the door. "I'm Zham Sa-Yool. There was some kind of mix-up about fueling?"

"No mix-up," Stanley said officiously. "The fuel pump is occupied."

"By whom?"

"Who do you think?" groused the stationmaster, nodding at the only other ship in the dock.

"They don't seem to be fueling, though," Zham said.

"That doesn't change the fact that they have reserved the pump," Stanley said. "I have the relevant forms on file."

"How long is their reservation?" Zham said.

"It can be extended," the stationmaster said, "at my discretion."

There was a long silence. Niko broke it by slapping her thigh.

"Got it!" she said. "This is a shakedown, right? He wants a bribe."

"Probably," Zham said patiently. "But it's not considered polite to say so out loud."

"Listen, kid," the stationmaster growled. "It's not a shakedown, because, first of all, that would be illegal under the Aur Lunach Military Code, punishable by no less than five years in prison and/or expulsion from the service, and *second* of all because no bribe you could offer me is going to outbid what the Anarks already paid. Understand?"

"They pay that well?" Niko said.

"It's partly that," the stationmaster said, "and partly that they've got the heaviest artillery within a thousand klicks. Always worth taking into account."

"They threatened you?" Zham said.

"Didn't have to. Everyone knows all Anarks are crazy. It's that shit they drink, gives 'em strange ideas."

"So, when can we get our fuel?" Zham said, grinding his teeth.

"Whenever Harry Gough says you can," the stationmaster said. "Or when he runs out of money, but I wouldn't fuckin' hold my breath."

"Who's Harry Gough?"

"Mr. Gough," said a new voice with a twangy Anark accent, "is the captain of the *Move Fast & Break Things*, as well as the president of Gough Resource Extraction LLC."

Zham turned. A dark-skinned, shaven-headed man in a sleeveless white shirt, a long black tie, and torn, fading jeans occupied the doorway. His arms were covered in complex interlocking tattoos, all thick black lines connected by intricate scrawl.

"Is that you?" Niko said.

He chuckled. "I'm afraid not. But Mr. Gough has asked me to say that he is most desirous of meeting with a passenger of yours, a Ms. Xenia Oserova."

"Of course he is," Zham said. "But I doubt she wants to see him."

"Mr. Gough is certain she will. He desires only a few minutes to discuss some matters of mutual interest. And afterward, I believe our fueling needs will be at an end."

Zham threw a look at the stationmaster, who threw up his hands in a *leave me out of it* gesture. The Anark smiled. He was missing a half dozen teeth, and those that remained were brown and stained.

"You don't have to do this," Zham said.

"From the sound of it, I do, or we're never getting out of here," Xenia said. She fixed her bun in place with a long metal pin and looked at herself in the mess hall mirror. Satisfied, she straightened her tie and picked up her black leather bag. "It's only a meeting. What's the worst that could happen?"

"He could kidnap you, drag you back to his ship, torture you until you give up the location of the valley, and dump you over the side," Zham said promptly. The thought had been rather preying on his mind.

Xenia rolled her eyes. "This is still *civilization*, Zham. You can't just do that sort of thing."

"It's a pretty thin kind of civilization, this far from anything," Zham said. "And you don't know Anarks." Not that Zham did, really. But in his current jumpy state, he was inclined to believe the worst of the rumors.

"I doubt even Anarks would risk war with the Academies, no matter how rich the prize."

"It's only a risk if the Academies find out," Zham said darkly. It was mostly to himself, though, since she'd obviously made up her mind. "We're coming with you, at least."

"I wouldn't turn down the escort," she said, and her smile had the faintest quiver that hinted at the state of her nerves. Zham reminded himself that in spite of her impressive composure, Xenia was new to life outside her library.

Back at the docking hatch, Niko had organized the troops. Zham would have felt vastly better if Ingeborg had been among them, but she'd apparently disappeared into the engine deck without a word, and there wasn't time to track her down. Instead, he'd have to make do with the forces available, which consisted of Niko herself, Aoife, and Lanzo, with Elli and Anni's participation vetoed by their father in spite of their enthusiastic pleading. Weapons, in theory, were not allowed on the station; this would have made Zham more comfortable if he were certain the rules applied to well-heeled Anarks.

Arranged in a flying wedge with Xenia at the center, they went in. The station's habitation level—surprisingly small; most of the bulk was machinery and storage for food and fuel—featured a sad little bar, not much more than an open space by a window with some cheap metal furniture and a tiny bartop. A couple of doors led to private dining rooms, though from the look of the place, Zham wasn't eager to sample the cuisine.

Two tables had been dragged together near the bar and hosted a half dozen Anarks. Like the messenger, they wore jeans and sleeveless shirts in various states of disrepair. Hairstyles tended toward the wild on both men and women, with spikes and shaved patches. They all bore tattoos on their arms and sometimes their faces as well, mostly in the same black-line style, though an occasional patch of color stood out. At the center of the table stood a large bowl of fizzing, bubbling liquid, into which several empty bottles of alcohol had evidently been poured. There were no guns in evidence, which made Zham feel a little better.

"We're looking for Gough," he said, staring among the tattooed faces to determine who was in charge.

"Mr. Gough is waiting inside," an unexpected voice said. At the bar, Erich Aur-Brahda unfolded his lanky frame from a stool and gave a stiff nod. "Mr. Sa-Yool, a pleasure to see you again. Although I am disappointed you chose to ignore my advice."

"I can be unpredictable that way," Zham said. "But I didn't take you for an Anark."

There was a round of ugly laughter from the table. Erich only shrugged.

"I am a sell-stick, the same as you. My current contract is with Gough Resource Extraction, for airborne security and . . . other services." He bowed slightly deeper toward Xenia. "You must be Ms. Oserova."

"I am," Xenia said, only the slightest tremble in her voice. "If you can let Mr. Gough know I've arrived?"

"Mr. Gough can see that for himself." Another Anark emerged from the dining room. He was short and well-muscled, with slick, dark hair, pale blue eyes, and a too-wide smile of blinding whiteness. He wore a pale blue linen coat and slacks, his shirt collar unbuttoned to show a hint of hairy chest. "Welcome."

"What is it you would like to discuss?"

Gough gave a belly laugh. "Haw! Straight to the point, I like that. But what business you and I have, m'dear, is best discussed in private." He gestured to the dining room. "Shall we?"

Xenia's eyes flicked momentarily to Zham. His jaw tightened. Through the open doorway he could see the small room was empty, but still . . .

"We'll stay right here," he muttered into her ear. "If you need us, just shout."

Xenia gave a decisive nod and stepped forward. "As you like, Mr. Gough."

Gough reached out and took her hand, ignoring the slight flinch this provoked. "Erich, mind the rest of our guests. They can kick back and relax. Bar's on me. Haw!"

"As you wish, Mr. Gough." Zham fancied he could detect the tiniest sneer curling Erich's aristocratic lip. He turned back to Zham and gestured to another table. "Please, sit."

Reluctantly, Zham sat, and his companions followed suit. Lanzo was staring after Gough with a hard frown on his face, while Aoife looked at Zham.

"You feel good about this?" she said.

"No," Zham admitted.

"Think we ought to have run it by Quedra?"

"She asked me to take care of it," Zham said. He really, really hoped that wouldn't turn out to be a horrible mistake.

"Some of them have the same tattoos," Niko said, apropos of nothing. She was staring at the Anarks, apparently immune to embarrassment. "Do they mean something, do you think?"

"Corporate logos," Aoife said. Her voice had a strange tone. "They get paid to show them off. All the proles have them."

Zham blinked. Aoife's accent sounded Anark sometimes, though not as harsh as Gough's, but he'd never asked her about it. Any time she'd referred to her past, which wasn't often, it was always in the Empire.

"What, so, it's like advertising?" Niko said.

"Sort of a combination between that and cattle-branding," Aoife said. Her expression said that she regretted bringing it up, but Niko bulled ahead regardless.

"That's so strange," she said. "Is that where you grew up? What was—"

"She doesn't like to talk about it," Lanzo said quietly.

"It's all right," Aoife said, laying her hand on his. "I don't. But the short answer is that my parents ran away from Anarkos when I was a baby. I grew up in Aur Paarva with their stories."

"Oh," Niko said, belatedly reading the emotion at the table. "Sorry. I get interested and then—"

Thankfully, she was interrupted by the bartender, a mousy young man in gray, who appeared unasked to deposit a pitcher of watery beer and four not-really-clean glasses on the table.

"Lovely," Aoife said, pouring herself some regardless.

When the bartender had scuttled back to the safety of his bartop, another figure was standing over them. One of the Anarks, a big woman with a floppy curl of hair dyed brilliant green, looked down at the four of them like a scientist studying a hitherto-undiscovered tapeworm. When she caught Zham's eye, she smiled wide; her teeth were as brown as Gough's were brilliant.

"Something I can do for you?" Zham said.

"Don't mind me," she said. "Just trying to figure out how you Imps can drink that piss."

"It's not my favorite," Zham admitted. "Hard to get good beer all the way out here, I guess. Have you ever been to Aur Marka? There's a brewery there—"

"You want a real drink?" she said, beckoning to her companions. There was a round of sniggers. One of the Anarks dipped a mug into the bubbling bowl and brought it over. "Here. Have a taste."

"I'm not in the mood for drinking, I'm afraid," Zham said, glancing toward the dining room. "We're just waiting—"

"I'll try it!" Niko said.

"Girl's got balls, even if she's got no tits," the woman said, to a round of laughter from the others. Zham's jaw tightened, but Niko cheerfully reached for the mug and took a swallow. Her eyes went very wide for a moment.

"That's . . . whew," she said. "Some drink."

The Anark looked challengingly at Zham. He glared back at her as he accepted the mug from Niko. A sip of the dark-colored liquid made him wince—it was cloyingly sweet, and the bubbles stung his nostrils, while alcohol bit hard at the back of his throat. He made a point of holding it in his mouth for a moment, meeting the woman's stare, before he spat it on the metal floor.

"Sorry," he said, handing the mug back. "Not to my taste."

"Stick with your *beer*, then," she said. "Still looks like piss to me."

"Or garbage water," said the man who'd brought the mug. "Did you bring that over from your ship? She looks like a garbage scow to me."

Lanzo and Aoife tensed in their seats. Zham held up a hand.

"She's old, I'll grant," he said. "But she does well enough."

"Well enough to haul trash and plug bugs, maybe," the woman said. "Is it true that you Imps fuck the mantids as well as eating them? Gives a new meaning to a dinner date." There was much guffawing at this witticism, and the others from their table joined in.

"I heard Imps can't get it up without a shot of bugblood."

"Is it true Imp girls get mantid claws down there instead of hair?"

"The Prez was saying that your ship's ready to fall out of the sky," the man with the mug said. "Says you've got kids working on it 'cause you can't find anybody better." This got another round of laughter. "Your aeros won't fly, your engineer's an old coot"—he raised his hands, building to a triumphant climax—"and your captain's a crippled bi—"

At this point, his nose shattered beneath Zham's knuckles with an extremely satisfying *crunch*.

Zham had been in a few bar fights. More than a few, actually, enough that he'd formulated his own Rules for Inebriated Fisticuffs. Rule Number One: Never pick a fight with anyone bigger than you. Rule

Number Two: Never pick a fight with anyone who has a bunch of friends along. Rule Number Three: Try to be good and drunk before you start, so it'll hurt less.

Right at the start, then, he'd violated all three principles. The Anark was shorter than him but broader and considerably more muscular, and he had a whole table of friends. Probably that meant Zham was about to have a very bad time, but there are certain comments you just can't let pass.

The Anark woman swung for him, but he was ready for it and she was still off-balance. Her fist whistled past the side of his head, while his slammed deep in her gut, doubling her over. The guy with the broken nose—it clearly was not his first time with that designation—roared and lowered his head to charge like a bull, only to be tackled from the side by Lanzo. Aoife, in spite of being enclosed in an acre of ruffles, was apparently still quite capable of throwing a punch that snapped another Anark's head right back.

After that, things went somewhat less well, because they were four—well, three and a girl the size of a wet rat—against six fighting-mad bruisers. Zham landed another punch, felt someone club him from behind, and stumbled into the embrace of a grinning Anark, who pinioned his arms. Broke-nose lined up for some free hits, but he was intercepted again, this time by Niko. Zham rapidly revised his opinion of her combat value; even without a handy baguette, she wrapped herself around the man from behind, legs cinched at his waist, one arm around his throat. His flailing fist caught her in the head hard enough to make Zham wince, but she hooked her fingers in his squashy nose and pulled back until he screamed.

Zham snapped his head back, slamming against the woman holding him and possibly adding another nose to his tally. She let go and he stumbled away toward where Aoife was trading blows with two Anarks and getting the worst of it. A double-handed blow to the back of the head sent one of them flopping onto the table, spilling the pitcher of beer. Before Zham could do something about the other, a kick out of nowhere caught him low in the chest. He staggered away, wheezing, and watched as Lanzo grabbed an Anark, wound up for a punch, realized it was a woman, hesitated, and got kneed in the balls for his troubles.

That left one on Aoife, a woman standing over Lanzo and cracking her knuckles, and a pair closing in on Zham, who had yet to regain his breath. Off to one side, Niko's victim was still giving desperate bellows, and another Anark lay groaning where he'd rolled off the table. They'd given a good account of themselves, Zham reckoned as he tried to raise his fists, but this was going to hurt—

"Oh!" Ingeborg said from the doorway. "Fun."

Those two words were the whole of her dialogue—probably for the day—but by the way she shrugged out of her coat and dropped into a fighting crouch, the Anarks deduced she was there to join the party. One of Zham's opponents broke off to face this new threat, swinging a wild roundhouse punch that caught nothing but air. Ingeborg sidestepped, *fast* in spite of her bulk, and punched him so hard, he spun three times in the air before he hit the ground.

At that point it was all hands on deck, with the three upright Anarks charging in together. Zham, wobbling like a drunk, felt like he ought to join in, maybe hit someone from behind, but it was quickly apparent his efforts would be superfluous. At one point, Ingeborg had an Anark in each hand and was banging them together like a toddler making her dolls kiss. When everyone was on the ground and seemed to be staying there, she ambled over to Zham and held out a hand to help him up.

"Thanks," Zham wheezed, and coughed. "Everyone else okay?"

"There's blood all *over* my dress," Aoife complained.

Lanzo, still writhing with one hand clutching his privates, raised the other in a shaky thumbs-up.

"Get her off!" an Anark screamed. "Oh gods my eyes!"

"You'd better go rescue that one from Niko," Zham said.

Ingeborg gave an affirmative grunt and headed over. Zham tested his own nose gingerly—bleeding, but it didn't seem to be broken—and wiped at his sodden upper lip. He looked up at the bar and found Erich looking back at him. The nobleman raised a small glass of whiskey in salute.

"What is going on out here?" The voice was Gough's but the surprise was insincere, as though it were a line he'd rehearsed. If he was supposed to be responding to the noise, Zham thought, it was a little late. The door to the dining room opened. "Has something—"

He stopped, eyes widening in genuine shock. Zham figured it was supposed to be the *Last Stop* crew who were lying bruised on the floor at this point.

"Just a small altercation," Erich said, tossing back his whiskey and getting to his feet. "Some of the crew expressed their opinions on Imperial culture, and matters grew . . . heated."

"I can see that."

Xenia appeared behind Gough, to Zham's relief, and pushed past him out of the room. "If you'll excuse me."

"You should, uh, really consider my offer," Gough said, now evidently off his script. "If you'd like to come aboard ship, we can talk—"

"I've heard all I care to," Xenia said haughtily. "Good day."

"I'll tell the stationmaster to connect us to the fueling pump, shall I?" Zham said, wiping another string of blood from his nose. "I understand you're done with it."

"Yeah," Gough said sourly, looking across his groaning crew. "I suppose I am."

"Xenia," Zham said. "Slow down."

"What?" She looked around, as though roused from a daze, and slowed her stalking pace to a walk. "Sorry. Are you all right?"

"Peachy," Zham said, spitting blood on the deck. "Are you?" Xenia didn't seem injured, but she was clearly furious. "Did Gough—I mean, did he try anything untoward?"

"I should say so!"

"Fucker." Zham felt his own fury rise with surprising speed. He stopped, looking back to the bar. "I'll kill him. Just wait here—"

She looked at him, eyebrows knitted for a moment, then her eyes widened.

"Oh! Not—nothing like *that.*" Her lip quirked. "Though I'm glad you're so eager to defend my honor."

"Then I'm confused."

"He asked me come aboard his ship and guide him to the valley. Offered me money." She snorted. "As though I would betray the Academies for *coin.* The professor has entrusted me with this assignment, and I intend to see it through."

"Ah," Zham said, hackles lowering a little. "I figured it would be . . . something like that."

"You expected this?"

"Not exactly. But the Imperial, Erich, approached me in Aur Lunach. Tried to buy your secret and then warned me off. I guess he was already working for Gough."

"The professor was circumspect when he made his inquiries, but I suppose someone else could have put the pieces together," Xenia said.

"Maybe," Zham said.

The others, who'd fallen a little behind Xenia's pace, were now catching up. She turned to address them with a slight flush in her cheeks.

"You've all gotten yourselves hurt for my sake," she said. "I'm very grateful for your bravery."

"The very least I can do," Lanzo said, still walking with a slightly widened gait.

"The way they were coming on, we didn't have much choice," Aoife said. "If Zham hadn't hit that bastard, I was getting close."

"I suspect we were intended to," Zham said. "Gough was trying to get Xenia to jump ship. If she came out and found us all in a heap, maybe he'd argue that we couldn't do the job."

"Silly," Ingeborg grunted.

"It sounds like his kind of trick," Xenia said. "I'm just glad nobody was seriously injured."

"Thankfully, Ingeborg came along when she did," Zham said.

"Anni found me eventually," Ingeborg said. "Was busy on the ship. Thought I saw something on the engine deck, had to make sure it was locked down."

"Something?" Aoife said. "Like an intruder?"

Ingeborg shrugged.

"Where'd you learn to fight like that?" Zham said to Niko.

She grinned at him, in spite of what was developing into a truly impressive black eye. "I have brothers as well as sisters, and they were always bigger than me."

"Do your brothers still have their eyes and noses?"

Niko smiled wider. "Only because I like them."

It was getting late in the day, and the *Last Stop* was outlined against the faintly glowing western horizon by the time they reached the dock. Quedra was waiting, cane in hand and Martin by her side, when the battered group filed through the hatch. She looked them over and gave an impressed whistle.

"Some party," she said, looking at Zham. "Anything I need to worry about?"

"There was a little trouble over the fueling schedule," Zham said, drawing himself up. "We handled it."

Quedra stared at him levelly for a couple of heartbeats, then nodded and turned away. Zham felt a grin spread across his face.

CHAPTER
SEVEN

We're out of fuel," Sev said.

Quedra looked from the old engineer to Zham, eyes hooded.

They were on the bridge in the brightness of early morning above the Layer, two days south from Theovan. Sev had made the trip up from the engine deck to request this meeting, a rare occurrence indeed. They were joined at the map table by Quedra, Zham, Karl, and Ingeborg, while Martin stood by the controls. The other pilots, Zham had no doubt, were listening just outside the door.

"I was under the impression," Quedra said, "that we'd topped off the tanks at Theovan."

"The gauge still shows nearly full," Martin said.

"Ain't surprised," Sev said, "considerin' it's wedged in place down below. There's a cut in one of the lines leading to number two, and the valve is jimmied open. Our bugblood's been drizzlin' into the Layer since we left."

"That's not a maintenance failure or a mistake, then," Karl said, alarmed. "That's deliberate sabotage."

"Yup," Sev said. "Neat, too. A nice slow leak, not so much we'd notice right away. Best I reckon, someone wanted us to run out of juice right about here."

"It has to be the Anarks, doesn't it?" Zham burst out. "Gough and his crew."

"Knew I saw something," Ingeborg muttered. Her knuckles were showing white; she took her security duties seriously.

"Must have been on his way out," Sev said. It was, as ever, hard to read their expression beneath goggles and mustache. "Fault's mine as much as anyone's. We checked the deck together, and I didn't spot nothin' wrong."

"Fault isn't important," Quedra said. "What matters is what we can do about it. What are our options?"

"We can still reach Theovan by radio, and they can relay a signal back to Aur Lunach," Karl said. "We can contract someone to come out here and get us moving."

"That'll take weeks," Zham said. "Assuming Gough hasn't bribed someone to lose our messages."

"Assuming we could afford it," Quedra said. "We're in the middle of nowhere; nobody's coming out here unless they're well paid."

"And the only ship we know is in the area is the *Move Fast & Break Things*," Zham said. "I can probably guess what Gough's price would be."

"If we have to turn back and try again, that'll give him a chance to search for himself," Karl said. "Just by being here, we've narrowed it down a lot for him."

"So, we'd rather not wait for help," Quedra summed up. "What else can we try?"

"The aero fuel tanks are still full," Karl said. "I checked just this morning."

"Can't burn that in the main engines," Sev said. "Not unless you want 'em wrecked 'fore nightfall."

Karl's lips moved for a moment in soundless calculation. "With drop tanks, the Krager can make it to Theovan from here. We could have Aoife pick up some fuel—"

Sev was already shaking their head. "Like spittin' in a well. It'd take a dozen trips to even get us back to the station."

"Seems pretty obvious to me," Zham said. "We still have that distiller in the hangar, right?"

Everyone stared at him.

"Aye," Sev said after a moment. "Haven't run it in years, but I expect I could get it going."

"Then all the fuel we need's just a few klicks that way," Zham said, pointing straight down. "We just have to take the descender and pick it up."

There was another silence. Quedra's lip twisted.

"The juice from a dozen cows would fill the tanks," Karl said cautiously. "But . . ."

"We've done it before," Zham said. "Drop quiet, get what we need, and get out without causing a swarm. Ingeborg, you know the trick of it, right?"

Ingeborg grunted affirmatively.

"And you'd be willing to try?" Quedra asked her.

Another grunt.

"If somethin' goes wrong, they'll have no support," Sev said. "Can't have an aero on station that low, and it'd take minutes to get down from *Last Stop.*"

"I can rig the Krager with a lev tank in place of an auxiliary fuel tank," Karl said. "It'll cut maneuverability, but then it can stay by the descender."

"Zham," Quedra said. "This was your idea. You're up for it?"

"Of course," Zham said. "I'll take the Krager. I'll need a tail gunner, and Ingeborg will need . . . say two more hands?"

Ingeborg nodded. Karl gave a sigh.

"It'll have to be me," he said. "The piping will all be jury-rigged; it may need fixing on the fly."

"I'm not making anyone do this," Quedra said. "We can always wait to be rescued."

"And maybe not get paid, right?" Karl said. "I want the *Last Stop* to keep flying as much as anybody. For the girls, it's home."

* * *

Aoife agreed to be the third person on the descender team, while Niko enthusiastically volunteered to be Zham's backseat. After a furious few hours banging equipment into shape, the aero was ready, while Sev and Lanzo kept working to get the distiller cleaned and functioning. Zham sat in the unfamiliar cockpit of the Krager-7a, hastily reviewing the cheat sheet Aoife had scrawled for him.

Niko was in the rear seat, facing backward at the controls of a rotating machine-gun mount. Her voice came to Zham through his headset. "No offense, but if Aoife's coming along, shouldn't it be her up there? This is her aero."

"I've done this kind of thing before," Zham said. "And she said, quote, 'If you're going to strap a big fat lev tank to the belly, I'd rather walk.'"

Niko snorted a laugh. Zham found the autoignition switch at last, put a thumb on it, and flipped the radio on.

"Ready to go in the Krager."

"You're clear," Martin said from the tower. "Good luck."

Off to one side of the flight deck, Elli and Anni jumped up and down and waved. Xenia stood with them, offering a small wave of her own. Zham waved back, glad his blush was hard to see at this distance.

"So," Niko said, uncharacteristically tentative. "Uh. Hypothetically."

"Hypothetically what?"

"Never mind. I'll tell you later."

"Niko."

"Later! Mission first. Let's goooooo!"

Zham sighed and pushed the switch. The Krager's two big engines coughed and sputtered to life, propellers whipping into an invisible blur. Zham eased the throttle forward and the aero started to move.

Last Stop had descended below the Layer and now hovered a few kilometers up, just high enough that flying mantids were unlikely to trouble her. That still left plenty of air beneath them, so Zham let the Krager glide off the end of the deck and down into a gentle circling dive as he got a feel for the aero's handling. The bolt-on tank carrying pressurized liquid lev made the aero feel heavy and sluggish, as though it were twice its normal weight. Fortunately, on this mission, tight maneuvering was unlikely to be required.

Once they were below the *Last Stop*, Zham could see the ship's rarely used belly hatch opening. The descender slowly emerged. It looked for all the world like a fishing line with a cylindrical weight on the end, dropping straight down like a sinker heading for the depths. This was a little deceptive—the line paying out from the *Last Stop* was just there to guide the little craft back in and was far too thin to support its bulk. The "weight," the body of the descender, was big enough to contain several hastily repurposed fuel tanks plus Ingeborg, Karl, Aoife, and their equipment, as well as a large integral lev tank that lowered it slowly and, hopefully, would raise it again.

"Can you guys hear me okay?" Zham said, punching to another channel.

"Loud and clear," Aoife said. "Get down there and find us a good spot."

"On it," Zham said.

They circled lower, through a few wispy clouds, and the jungle below started to come into focus. The Krager had a bombsight that allowed Zham to look straight down, handy for examining the terrain. He stared at the endless sea of thick green leaves and interwoven branches. Every square inch of ground that could support the big jungle trees was occupied as they endlessly struggled to outreach one another and soak up the diffuse sunlight that made it through the Layer.

"What are we looking for?" Niko said.

"Clearings," Zham said. "The mantids make them. Knock down a few trees, undergrowth springs up, plenty for the cows to eat."

"Clever bastards."

"Unfortunately," Zham said. "How come you were so eager to come down here, anyway?"

"Seemed like fun!" Niko said. "When I was a kid, we would look down at the jungle while we waited for hunters to drop off their catch. I always wondered what it was like down there."

"Hot," Zham muttered. "And the air's wrong. You'll see."

"Is that a clearing off to the left?"

"Hang on." Zham banked to get a better look. "Looks fresh. Let's get overhead."

A quick pass confirmed it. Two dozen mantid cows like huge white ticks chewed placidly on the bright green undergrowth, undisturbed by the drone of the aero high overhead. Zham radioed the position to Ingeborg, and the descender moved sideways just above treetop height, propelled by a wide-bladed fan in a rotating mount like an ungainly balloon.

Speaking of balloons. Zham bled power from the engines to the lev tank, activating its internal heaters. The pressurized liquid lev boiled, enormously increasing its levity. He chopped the throttle to minimum and feathered the props, losing speed to well below the point where the aero would have fallen out of the sky under normal circumstances. However, like the scooter he'd ridden into the Aur Marka skies, the Krager and its lev tank were now light enough that they could float without the aid of lift.

The resulting vehicle, a weird crossbreed between an aero and a levship, was awkward in the extreme, but it let Zham hover in place a bare ten meters above the ground at the edge of the clearing. Karl had attached a rope ladder, and Zham slid the canopy back and let the ladder fall. The bottom rungs thumped into the tall grass.

Without prompting, Niko had her own canopy open, and she scrambled over the side and nimbly descended the ladder, unbothered by its swaying. When she reached the bottom, she pounded a couple of spikes into the ground with her boot and triggered their spring-loaded barbs. With the Krager tethered like an unruly goose, Zham was able to leave the engines running at minimum and climb down himself, somewhat more slowly. He did his best to ignore the weird sight of an aero hovering in place overhead.

Now that he was down—one nerve-racking task complete—the dubious pleasures of being in the green zone asserted themselves. The air felt *thick*, so heavy with moisture it was like breathing soup, hypersaturated with the scents of the jungle and a metallic ozone tang. He could almost feel a billion spores taking root in his lungs.

"Shallow breaths," he told Niko, "or you'll pass out. And don't forget to drink water." It was sauna-hot, and sweat already trickled down his forehead.

The descender had come to rest a dozen meters away, crashing through a few tree limbs to ground itself just beyond the clearing's edge. Ingeborg emerged first, carrying a big, short-barreled 0.8 cm machine gun in both hands with a trailing belt of ammunition leading to her pack. Aoife—she'd thankfully decided on flight suit over dress on this occasion—followed with Karl, equally cautious if less impressively armed.

"So, now—" Niko began.

Ingeborg held up a hand. "Wait."

They waited, breathing fast and shallow. The mantid cows made remarkably little sound for their vast size, with only the occasional creak of chitin and click of mandibles as they munched through grass and saplings. The trees rustled in the faint breeze, but there was none of the birdsong or animal calls you might hear in a mountainside forest. Down there, making too much noise meant attracting the attention of eusocial hyperpredators, and anything that valued its skin or carapace had evolved to live in silence.

After a minute of listening, Ingeborg lowered her hand.

"Clear," she said. "For now. Stay quiet. Follow."

She attached the big gun to the side of her pack and stalked across the clearing, unbothered by the weight. Zham and the others strung out behind her, Niko closest and Karl keeping well to the rear. Ingeborg approached one of the mantid cows, which chose that moment to turn toward them, its eight legs shifting lazily. Mouth-parts like an industrial shredding machine ripped a swathe of grass from the earth, roots and all, and ground it into pulp. A pair of pale, atrophied eyes stared out blindly.

"Kill quick and quiet," Ingeborg said. "Take too long, gives off panic pheromone, spooks others." She drew a machete from its sheath on her hip and sauntered up to the enormous thing. "Spot is here. Behind the third dorsal ridge." She tapped the place she meant with the end of her blade. "Take your time. It can't see or hear you. No brain, anyway."

She lined the weapon up, angled to slip between two carapace plates, and brought it down in one swift stab. It sank to the hilt with a *squelch*. The cow jerked, then sagged forward with a *thud*, all its legs going out from under it at once.

"Cut primary dorsal nerve column," Ingeborg said. "Dead instantly." She wiped her face with one sleeve, and Zham wasn't sure if it was the heat or the strain of speaking—he hadn't heard her say this many words in a day before. "Understand?"

"I'll get those hoses," Karl said. "Aoife, help me?"

"Can I do the next one?" Niko said.

Ingeborg pursed her lips. "Watch once more," she said, and started trudging toward the next cow.

* * *

Once the novelty of being on the ground wore off and discomfort dulled the edge of terror, what remained was hard, heavy work in the heat, all while feeling like a wet towel was wrapped around your head. The hoses were big bastards, five centimeters across and reinforced with wire. They ended in a perforated metal spike, which you jabbed as deep into the cow's body as you could. Most of the insect's colossal bulk was composed of fluid sacs storing the incredibly high-energy fluid humans inaccurately named bugblood. Left to themselves, they would eventually be guided back to a nest by their mantid handlers and purge themselves into its reserves.

These cows, of course, were going nowhere. Each carcass had several hoses attached, the descender's pumps churning busily to extract bugblood and fill the tanks. Zham watched his assigned hoses for any sign of slackening—once they'd drained all the fluid they could, they had to be jammed into another part of the corpse to puncture more sacs. The cow's bodies visibly shrank as the pumps worked, collapsing like ice sculptures in the summer heat and leaving Zham feeling like a mechanically assisted vampire.

"We're going to need one more," Karl said, checking the tank levels and looking out at the field of dead cows. They'd killed ten, about half the herd, and while Ingeborg's technique had been excellent, the remaining creatures clearly sensed something was up. They shifted anxiously, turning more often, even lumbering a few steps forward before settling down to chew more grass.

"I'll get it," Niko said. She had a machete in hand, dark to the elbows with the black ichor that was the cow's actual blood. "Ingeborg, that one?"

The big woman looked up and gave an affirmative grunt. Niko hustled over, setting herself just behind the cow's head with its grinding mouthparts and positioning the blade carefully behind the dorsal ridge.

"Niko, wait," Zham said. The cow was shifting uneasily, head swinging. "Niko!"

She didn't hear him in time. As she started to plunge the blade down, the big insect moved, swinging its massive head clumsily toward her. The machete strike went awry, glancing away in a shower of black blood. The side of the cow's head slammed into Niko, sweeping her off her feet to go sprawling in the dirt.

"Fuck!" Ingeborg shouted. She started to run.

Zham was already moving, and he was closer. Niko lay on her back, scrabbling away as the cow loomed over her with its serrated mouthparts churning. It was making a high-pitched whistling sound like a mortally wounded teakettle. While it couldn't see her, Zham could all too easily imagine it crushing Niko in sheer panic under one of those flailing legs, or bringing its mouth down and shredding flesh and bone—

He'd drawn his pistol, a heavy 1.1, before he'd really thought about what to do with it. As the cow lurched forward again, he lined up on the spot Ingeborg had pointed out and fired three times. The cow's plating cracked and splintered, throwing up gouts of black blood, and it gave a final screech before collapsing drunkenly to one side, legs still twitching.

Another second, and he skidded to his knees in the dirt beside Niko. She was staring at the dying bug, pupils blown way out and breathing much too fast for the dense air.

"Hey! Niko!" When she didn't respond, he grabbed her shoulder and turned her roughly to face him. "Look at me. You're okay. Slow down."

"I . . ." Her head wobbled, eyes fluttering. Zham grabbed the back of her neck to keep her upright. After a moment, she steadied, taking slow, deliberate breaths. "Holy *fuck*."

"My fault," Ingeborg said, striding over. "Should have done it myself." She gestured at Niko's sodden forearms. "Bugs can smell blood. Not panic pheromone but close."

Whether it was the pheromone or the sound, the rest of the cows were definitely alerted now. They were running, as best they were able, rising up on all eight legs in a queerly dainty gait to get as far away from the source of the problem as possible. Zham saw one collide headfirst with a tree, wobbling drunkenly before turning in another direction and charging onward.

"At least that was the last one we needed," Niko said weakly.

"We have to go," Ingeborg said, raising her voice. "Now."

"We don't have enough!" Karl shouted back. "We'll get stuck halfway back to Theovan and have to do it all over again."

Ingeborg ground her teeth. "How long?"

"Three minutes," Karl said. He and Aoife were already humping a roll of hose over to the freshly killed cow.

"Hurry," Ingeborg said. She stomped back to the descender. A moment later, the whine of the pump increased in pitch.

Zham held out a hand to Niko and hauled her to her feet. Aoife unshipped a rifle from her shoulder and checked the bolt while Karl jammed a second hose into the cow.

"Get the rest of the hoses back to the descender," the engineer instructed. "Then watch the tank and tell me when it reaches the mark."

Zham grabbed one unused hose and Niko another, rolling them up as fast as they could manage. It was still quiet all around, but there was a new tension in the air.

Ingeborg was frowning at the pump as though she could will it to work faster. Zham tossed the hoses aboard and found the tank gauge, which was still a hair below Karl's penciled mark. Out in the field, Aoife raised the rifle to her shoulder and turned in a slow circle, then snapped round.

"Something's coming!" she shouted.

The brush at the edge of the clearing had started to thrash. She lined up on it, staring over the sights.

The creature that emerged didn't seem worth all the worry, at least at first. It looked like a beetle the size of a large dog, with a long shiny carapace of iridescent green with brown splotches. It moved on eight legs like the cows, and its color darkened toward the head, ending in a black spike on its nose like a rhino's horn. For a moment it stood stock-still, tasting the air, three gleaming black eyes staring out from either side of its head.

"Slave-soldier," Ingeborg muttered. "A scout. Careful . . ."

With a *scree* like a band saw spinning up, the beetle splayed its wing cases, two sets of shimmering wings whipping into a blur. It charged, head down and horn forward, wings lifting its abdomen partly off the ground so its legs seemed to be gripping the turf and hurling it forward rather than bearing its weight. It was shockingly fast, covering half the distance to Aoife between blinks.

She waited a heartbeat, choosing her moment, then fired, the rifle's *crack* as flat and hard as a slap. Chitin exploded from the beetle just left of its horn. Its legs spasmed and its head dropped far enough to bury the horn in the dirt, momentum flipping it head over arse with a spray of black blood. It crashed to the ground, wings crushed and broken, legs flailing wildly.

"*Run!*" Ingeborg bellowed.

The tank gauge had reached the mark. Karl planted his foot on the dead cow, yanked the hose out, and started rolling it up.

"Leave it!" Ingeborg swore and unshipped her machine gun. To Zham she spat, "Get to the aero!"

There was more thrashing at the edge of the clearing, a lot more. One *scree* sounded, then another.

Zham ran, Niko trailing behind him at first but quickly pulling ahead. He waved her on—she'd climb faster, anyway—and fought the stitch in his side and the air that pulled like thick glue at his lungs. Aoife was backing toward the descender, Karl still carrying the hose beside her.

"Fucking *run right now!*" Ingeborg yelled.

A dozen beetles broke from the brush. Aoife fired hastily, missed, and turned to sprint for the descender. Karl, finally getting the message, threw the hose aside and followed.

Ingeborg stepped past them, gun braced against her midsection. The noise when she opened fire was incredible, a vast *braaaaaaaap* like a monstrous sewing machine. Bullets tore one beetle to shreds, shifted in a *pock pock pock* line across the turf to the next and brought it down in a spray of blood and chitin. Brass spewed out of the gun's breech in a torrent, the ammo belt sucked into the other side just as quickly. Recoil hammered at Ingeborg, her muscles bulging with the effort of containing it.

Niko had reached the rope ladder and scrambled up like a monkey toward the hovering aero. Zham kicked the switch to free the spike from the dirt and started after her. A beetle was charging him, and he yanked his legs up just in time for it to speed past, knocking the lower rungs of the ladder aside. Free of the ground, it began to swing, the world shifting nauseatingly around him.

"Come on come on come on!" Niko yelled. She was clutching the grip of the tail gun, but with the aero level, it couldn't bear on the ground.

Back at the descender, beetles lay strewn in front of Ingeborg while Aoife stood in the hatchway with her rifle, shooting at fresh insects emerging from the trees. On the other side of the clearing, much closer to the descender, something big was coming out of the brush.

"Aoife! Ingeborg! Behind you!" Zham shouted.

The two women didn't hear over the sound of gunfire, but Niko did, and she relayed his warning through the radio. A moment later, Ingeborg turned just in time to see a mantid warrior step into the open.

This shape Zham recognized, if only from his nightmares. It was bright green and three meters high, though much of its bulk was in a horizontal abdomen riding low to the ground on four joined legs. Its upper body bore four more limbs, two heavily armored and shaped like scythes and two smaller ones beneath them with finger-like manipulators at the ends. A long neck supported a diamond-shaped head, dominated by a pair of glittering red compound eyes and half-meter-long mandibles that clacked like scissors. Two segmented antennae were never still, quivering with each slight movement.

Ingeborg started shooting immediately, the clatter of brass against the descender's hull drowned out by the roar of the gun. The mantid staggered as though walking into a heavy wind, and sparks showered from its hardened carapace. It came forward, mandibles clacking, jerking as a lucky shot caught a knee joint and ripped the lower half of one leg away. It didn't fall.

The descender started to rock, then lurched slowly into the air. A second mantid charged out of the jungle just as Ingeborg's weapon finally jammed, the end of the barrel glowing a dull red. She swore and grabbed Aoife's outstretched hand, swinging into the hatch as the descender left the ground. Aoife leaned past and fired her rifle, working the bolt with expert speed, but the bullets barely made an impression. She fell backward and slammed the hatch closed as the second mantid arrived. Its claws screeched down the metal of the hull as the descender continued to rise out of its reach.

"Turn turn turn!" Niko said, howling in frustration. Zham finally grabbed the edge of the canopy and hauled himself into the cockpit. He tweaked the throttle, ramping up one engine and throwing the Krager into a slow spin that unmasked Niko's tail gun. Almost immediately, the roar of the weapon hammered at Zham's ears, physically painful until he clawed his headgear on. Red tracers slashed across the field as she walked the stream of fire into the mantid. The heavier slugs of the 1.3 cm gun chewed away at it, tearing off chunks of its abdomen, but it still managed to swipe at the descender and leave a shiny scratch on the dull metal.

Then, finally, the ungainly craft was high enough to be beyond the mantids' reach. More beetles and mantid warriors started to fill the clearing, and Niko swung the gun around.

"Save your ammo!" Zham shouted over the intercom as he strapped himself in. "We're not through yet."

Fliers. Zham knew them from a very *specific* nightmare. *Tell Zham that I wish he'd asked me out sometime.* At the moment, they were just dots rising out of the jungle, but his mind painted the full picture, a mantid with its body stretched horizontally to four meters or more, trailing spindly, almost vestigial limbs and borne aloft by two pairs of huge iridescent wings. The mandibles were the same, like vast shears, and they could *spit* a sizzling acidic stuff that would eat through metal and flesh. He could imagine the splatter of impact, the cough of a failing engine, descending into the jungle—better to crash than to bail out—

Focus, he told himself. *Quedra asked if you could handle this. Handle it.* The danger wasn't to the Krager—no insect, however terrifying, could fly faster than the fighter-bomber's big Graufen engines—but to the descender, which could only continue its slow rise. Keeping it safe was why he and Niko were there.

Zham throttled all the way up and tweaked the props, the whirring blades clawing at the air. His eye was glued to the airspeed gauge, watching as it crept toward the magic number where there would be enough air over the wings to hold them aloft. It was like takeoff in some ways, albeit a wobbly, awkward takeoff at the mercy of the winds. The buoyancy of the lev tank made it impossible to maneuver properly, and he had to crane his head to spot the approaching fliers. They were already too close.

As soon as he felt the first sluggish touch of lift through the control stick, he jammed the purge switch on the lev tank. Hot levgas hissed out in a torrent, replaced with ordinary air, and abruptly the force of gravity applied to the Krager again. There was a stomach-turning lurch downward as the wings took the plane's weight, struts groaning. Zham yanked the stick back as hard as he dared, fighting for altitude.

"They're coming in fast," Aoife said over the radio. "Zham, where are you?"

"Getting there," Zham said through gritted teeth, the steep climb pushing his heart into his guts.

"Next time, *I* fly the aero!"

"I thought you didn't like having the lev tank on," Niko said, ever cheerful.

"It's better than sitting helpless in a tin can!"

They were level with the descender now. Zham kept climbing a moment longer, straightening out above the cylindrical craft on its long cable. The fliers, a dozen or more, were coming in an elongated swarm of gleaming wings.

"Niko, get ready on the screamer," Zham said.

"Screamer? Where?"

"The thing attached to the window. There should be a lever." Unless Karl had forgotten it—Zham hadn't checked, stupid—

"Got it!" Niko said. "Tell me when."

"After you crank it, start shooting the fuckers."

Zham nosed down into a shallow dive. The fliers were focused on the descender—no surprise there; it was probably drenched in nasty bug pheromones now—and ignored the buzz of the aero. He picked his target, right in the center of the swarm, and watched it grow and grow in his gunsight.

"Now!" he shouted to Niko, and thumbed both buttons on the stick.

The Krager, in addition to a pair of 1.3 cm machine guns in the wings, had dual center-mounted 2 cm autocannons, taking advantage of the clear field of fire in front of the cockpit. The sound was different, audible even through his headset, the fast rip of the machine guns undergirded by a deeper thumping. The effect when they hit was gratifying, explosive shells burrowing into the mantid for a split second before detonating in miniature geysers of black fluid and shattered chitin. Overkill, certainly—the fliers were more lightly armored than their warrior counterparts, and their wings shredded easily—but Zham allowed himself a moment of grisly satisfaction. One flier didn't come close to evening the score, but every little bit helped.

As they shot past the mantids, another sound penetrated the cockpit, a shrieking warble that rapidly rose in pitch and volume to tooth-scraping levels. The device that produced it was a simple mechanical siren clipped to the outside of the rear canopy. However much mantids were attracted to their pheromones, they hated that sound more. In the rearview mirror, Zham saw every mantid in the swarm bank into a turn.

"Um, they're following us!" Niko sang out. "They're all following us. Is that supposed to happen?"

"All according to plan," Zham said. "Blast them!"

"Right!"

The chatter of the tail gun thumped underneath the ongoing siren. In the mirror, Zham could see red tracers stitching the sky like a tongue of flame. Niko screamed in delight as her bullets chewed through one mantid and sent it tumbling in a storm of broken pieces.

"Watch your ammo!" Zham shouted. "Aim for the wings; they're fragile."

"*Yeeeee*haw!" Niko screamed. He wasn't sure she'd heard.

Regardless, he had more to worry about. This was a complex dance—get too far away and some of the fliers would wander off and go back to attacking the descender. Let them get too close, of course, and they'd start melting the rudder. The bugs might be slower than the Kräger, but they could climb straight up, faster than any aero could manage. Whenever he gained altitude, they closed in.

It was working, though. They were far above the jungle now, and he could see the blocky shape of the *Last Stop*, still way above but growing fast. High enough and the fliers would break off, unable to keep aloft in the thinner air. And Niko kept whittling down their numbers—

"Zham!" Aoife shouted.

"Problem," Ingeborg cut in. The sound of claws on metal came over the radio.

Zham spotted the descender off to one side and swore. One of the fliers had gotten loose from the swarm and closed in, landing on the vehicle's hull. It slashed repeatedly at the wall with its foreclaws, but more dangerous was the stuff starting to drip from its mouth. Drops of foam spattered and raised hissing coils of smoke.

"Niko, hang on!" Zham said.

"What—"

Her voice shifted to a surprised whoop as Zham jammed the stick sideways, rolling the Kräger onto its back. The gray of the Layer was abruptly replaced overhead by the green of the jungle, and all the blood in his body seemed to drain into his head. A second later, he hauled back on the stick, bringing the nose down and the tail up. For a terrifying moment, they were headed straight down, his vision full of nothing but green. Then the nose started to come up again, pulling the Kräger out of its vertical dive several hundred meters lower and headed in the opposite direction.

The split-S was exciting but routine—the next bit was the hard part. The pursuing mantids could corner and dive much faster than the aero, and he was now passing directly under them. They stooped on him, turning in unison like a single organism. For half a second, their paths crossed, and the air was suddenly full of buzzing bugs and flying spit. Zham rolled one way to let a mantid shriek past, then back the other as a ball of foamy acid plummeted toward him.

Then they were through, the mantids pulling out of their dives beneath him and resuming their pursuit.

"We're smoking!" Niko said. "Right wing."

Zham glanced nervously at the thin trail of smoke and willed it to stop. It obediently did, a tiny bit of spatter that burned itself out. Much too close.

The descender was now ahead of them, flier still clinging to the hull. Zham lined it up, finger on the button.

"Zham," Aoife said. "You can hit it, right?"

"I can hit it," Zham said.

"We haven't got any armor here," Karl said grimly.

Zham swallowed. "I can hit it."

"He can hit it," Ingeborg said, apparently serene.

The mantid filled the gunsight. Zham jerked the stick, tipping the Krager's wing up so its belly faced the descender, and thumbed the button. Guns only, no cannons, the streams of tracer converging on the mantid's midsection and walking outward as he closed, pulling up at the last possible moment to curve away—

"Got it!" Niko said, pumping her fist. When Zham had the time to check his rearview, he saw the broken mantid sliding down and away. "Nice shooting!"

"Get back on the gun," Zham said. He swallowed hard and dove back toward the rest of the swarm.

Fortunately, that was nearly the end of it. He only had to make one more pass before the swarm dispersed, the remaining fliers turning away and buzzing back down toward their jungle. Zham waited until the descender was safely pulled into the *Last Stop*'s bowels before bringing the Krager around and setting down on the deck, as neatly as if he'd been off on a quiet patrol.

Only once the engines had stopped did his hands start shaking. Niko popped her canopy at once and practically vaulted over the side, but Zham stayed in his seat a moment longer, bent over his knees with his stomach roiling. He yanked off his headgear, ears still ringing in spite of the muffling headphones.

When he finally got out, he found a welcome party waiting for him: Sev, Martin, and—surprisingly—Quedra, leaning on her cane. He wasn't sure when he'd last seen his sister on the flight deck.

"You all right?" Sev said.

"Fine," Zham said. "Just a touch of the bad air. Everyone okay down below?"

"Ingeborg reported no injuries," Martin said. "And Karl is connecting the tanks to the distiller as we speak."

"We were watching from here," Quedra said. "That was sharp flying."

"It was *amazing*," Niko burst in, gesturing like a five-year-old on a sugar high. "We were like *vrew* and *pewpewpew* and the first one went down, and then they all came after us and I was like *bambambam* but then one got past us and Zham did a split-S like *freeeow* and—"

"We took a hit," Zham said. "Make sure Karl looks at the wing before Aoife goes up again. And Ingeborg saved all our asses on the ground, as usual."

"Noted." Quedra almost smiled, her eyes searching his face. "You're really all right?"

"A little queasy, and my ears hurt," Zham said, cracking his back ostentatiously. "But I'll be okay."

Quedra was quiet a moment, as though debating what to say. She settled on "Good" and turned away, leaning on her cane. Martin hovered close by her shoulder, ready to lend an arm.

Waiting behind her was Xenia, looking uncharacteristically diffident. She offered a tight smile.

"I understand congratulations are in order."

"We came back alive," Zham said. "Congratulations are always in order."

"I'm glad to hear it." She hesitated, then went on. "When they told me the mantids were swarming, I found myself . . . distressed."

"I can imagine," Zham said. She looked taken aback, and he clarified. "If we couldn't get more fuel, we'd have to call for help and limp back to Theovan. Your whole mission might have been abandoned. I'm sure the professor would be very disappointed."

"Ah." She coughed. "Yes. Your continued service to . . . the mission is appreciated."

"Glad to give good value for money." Zham grinned.

Xenia straightened her tie and stood up straighter. "I look forward to working with you further, Zham Sa-Yool."

"Likewise," Zham said, a bit nonplussed, as she turned abruptly away. With a shrug, he looked at Niko.

"There's still a tub of ice cream in the freezer," he said. "I think we deserve ice cream."

"Yeah." Niko stared after Xenia for a moment, then shook her head and flashed her infectious smile. "We *definitely* deserve ice cream."

CHAPTER EIGHT

"Zham? Are you in there? I really need to talk to you."

Zham mumbled something and rolled over in his bunk, chasing the fleeting remnant of a pleasant dream. The knocking at his door continued, and he reluctantly opened his eyes a fraction.

"Niko?"

"Yes!" she said. "I mean, yes, it's me."

"Is someone shooting at us?"

"No."

"Mantids on board?"

"Not that I know of."

Zham's eyes slid closed. "Then wake me up for dinner."

"Zham, *please*. It's important. Or at least I think it's important, and I don't know what to do, and I've been trying to figure it out for *days*—"

"All right, all *right*." He sat up and pulled on a not-too-filthy T-shirt. "Come in."

The door to his tiny room opened slowly, and Niko peeked around it as though she expected him to throw something. He rolled his eyes and beckoned her inside.

"Sorry," she said. "I've been driving myself a little crazy."

"I can see that," Zham deadpanned. "What's going on?"

"I don't— It's hard to explain. I mean, it's not *hard* to explain, but you're going to be mad and I don't want to tell you but I *have* to because not telling would be worse—"

"Okay. Slow down." He got up and guided her to a seat on the bunk. "Just say it, whatever it is." He had a sudden thought, and his brow furrowed. "You haven't fallen in love with me, have you?"

"What? Of course not." Zham winced inwardly at her confused expression. "This is *serious*. It's . . ." She hesitated, then blurted out, "It's about Xenia."

Xenia had in fact featured heavily in the dream Zham had so reluctantly abandoned, and he felt a little guilty about it, so her unexpected invocation made him start like he'd been caught at something. "What about her?"

"It seemed like things were going so well for you two, you were flirting after we got back—"

"We weren't flirting."

Niko rolled her eyes. "But then Elli said she read that Academics can do magic, and that Xenia probably had witch stuff in all those bags. And Anni didn't believe her, and I said there's no such thing as magic, really, but Elli swore there was and everything kind of went from there. So, really," she said virtuously, "it's Elli's fault."

"Niko," Zham said patiently, "Elli is *eleven*. You're an adult." He shook his head. "It sounds weird to say this, but I sometimes think those girls are a bad influence on you. What did you do?"

"We snuck into Xenia's room to look through her things."

"*Niko.*"

"Just a little! Just to see if there was anything weird. And there *was*."

"What, like a trunk full of pointed hats and broomsticks? A little eye of newt?"

"Not exactly." Niko swallowed. "I need you to come see. Because maybe I'm wrong, and I don't want to get anyone in trouble."

"I can't just barge into her room and ask to start going through her stuff."

"I've got everything ready," Niko said. "She'll never know we were there; I promise."

"No. This is ridiculous."

"*Please,* Zham. You have to do this. Otherwise, something really bad might happen."

He stared into her lost-puppy eyes, which seemed to be getting wider by the moment. Finally, against his better judgment, he muttered, "You have a plan, then?"

Zham had a plan too, in case they were caught—throw Niko under the bus and never look back. He'd worked out an elaborate story in his head to blame her for everything. The trouble was, Zham wouldn't have bought it himself, so it was hard to imagine Xenia accepting it as an excuse for someone rifling her things.

It had to be said that Niko's plot unfolded without a hitch. Elli and Anni, willing co-conspirators, presented themselves at Xenia's door and asked if she could come with them to the hangar deck to inspect a project. Xenia tried to demur, but the twins refused to take no for an answer, in the way of eleven-year-olds, and she ended up being dragged to the stairs by both hands. Everyone else was up above, so it was just a matter of opening the door. Still, Zham hesitated; there were no locks aboard ship, but the habits of respecting privacy in tight quarters were deeply ingrained. With a last look at Niko, he gave a sigh and went in.

The room they'd given her was bigger than Zham's, with space for a desk and chair in addition to the fold-out bunk. It still felt small, however, given the amount of luggage crammed into it. Several of the big trunks were open, pushed against the wall or under the desk. These were full of neatly labeled binders and bound stacks of paper, presumably part of the work the professor expected her to do while away. Another trunk contained a collapsible drying frame, now erect and laden with a variety of intimate garments. Zham looked away, reddening, but Niko immediately charged over.

"*This* wasn't here last time," she said, rubbing the fabric between her fingers. "Very nice."

"Niko."

She splayed her fingers inside the cups of a brassiere. "She's bigger than she looks, right? I think it's the suits."

"Niko!"

"I'd just like to see her in one of those backless Markan numbers, you know, they're black with sort of sequins— Okay!" Niko bent to the pile of luggage, smirking. "You can't say you wouldn't appreciate it, though."

Obviously, but that was neither here nor there. "If you brought me in to peek at her *underwear*, I'm going to hang you out the bridge window by your ankles."

"Come on," Niko said, still rummaging. "I wouldn't do that."

"You definitely would!"

"Okay, but I might feel bad about it afterward." She lifted one trunk out of the way, grunting with effort, and exposed another. It was larger than most, leather-bound with brass corners, and had a small keyhole. "This is the one."

"Is it locked?"

"It was," she said. "Anni opened it."

"Since when can Anni pick locks?"

"Since Elli taught her last summer, I think?" Niko pushed the trunk open with her foot. "There. Is that what I think it is?"

Zham stared down, throat going very tight.

"Yeah," he said slowly. "It sure looks like it."

The *Last Stop* flew south through clear skies. Squalls below the Layer made the clouds bubble up and glow with flashes of lightning, but little disturbed the sunlit tranquility up above. The maps grew sparser the farther they went, becoming vague suggestions of terrain.

Quedra ordered regular patrols in spite of the emptiness, but they caught no hint of the *Move Fast* or any other ship.

When they reached the last waypoint, Quedra summoned Xenia to the bridge. Zham was on watch, doing regular scans of the horizon with his binoculars. Down on the flight deck, Aoife was playing some kind of ball game with Elli and Anni, full Szacine dress swishing wildly.

Xenia knocked, and Zham hurried over to the door. Quedra was in her wheelchair today, and there was a tightness to her jaw that told Zham her pain was running high. For Quedra to concede even that much reaction was, for her, an unusual show of humanity.

"Good morning," Xenia said smiling. Zham tried to smile back, but unlike his sister, hiding his emotions had never been his strong suit. He saw Xenia's eyes narrow as she sensed something off in his expression.

"Morning," he said gruffly, stepping aside and gesturing to the map table.

"We've reached the last waypoint you gave us," Quedra said. "It's time for the final location."

It felt momentous, the revelation of this deadly secret they'd flown thousands of kilometers to find, but Xenia took it in stride. She bent over the map table, muttering a few numbers under her breath, and drew a short line with a ruler and a grease pencil.

"There," she said. "There are three tall peaks that look like they're in a line until you're right overhead. The valley is between them."

Quedra looked at the marking. "Zham, set a course and take us below the Layer. We should be there in an hour."

That hour was one of the longest of Zham's life. The *Last Stop* descended slowly, buffeted by the turmoil of the Layer for a few minutes before breaking out into the gray sky beneath. He swung wide to avoid a thundershower, lightning flashing out the starboard window, but after that, there was nothing to do but wait. The silence on the bridge grew and grew. Quedra didn't seem inclined to break it, lost in her contemplation of the map, and Zham didn't trust himself to speak to Xenia. Xenia in turn caught his mood, going from confused to frustrated to quietly furious and staring intently out the window to cover it.

The relief when Quedra called all spare hands to the bridge was palpable. Everyone but Sev and Martin crowded in, filling the space and fighting for spots at the windows. Niko pushed close to Zham's side, throwing her own glance at Xenia, and they exchanged a wordless look.

"Those are certainly mountains," Aoife said, voicing the general opinion.

There was no denying that much. Three steep-sided peaks, well frosted with snow, loomed amid a range of lesser hills. They rose well above the green zone, jungle petering out on the slope like the last strands of a balding man's hair and giving way to a zone of gray-brown grasses and then bare rock. To Zham's unpracticed eye they didn't look particularly valuable as real estate, too steep to build on without enormous effort.

As they approached, however, it became clear that Xenia's description was correct. The three mountains defined not a line but a narrow triangle, connected by saddles and ridgelines still high enough to be snowcapped. In between the ground fell steeply, and Zham could see a pocket of jungle alongside a splotch of yellow-green that had to be the algae-colored surface of a long, thin lake.

"That's . . . promising," Quedra said, an impressed note in her voice.

"It looks fully enclosed," Aoife said, pointing. "That's the lowest spot there, and it's still just rock."

"How big is it?" Lanzo said.

Karl pursed his lips. "Hard to say without proper measurements. But it has to be three or four times the size of Aur Lunach."

A new energy crackled through the room. Hearing about a place like this as a distant prospect was one thing; actually seeing it was quite another. It was the sort of thing every flier dreamed of finding.

"Steady on," Quedra said. "Victor must have gotten excited too, and we don't know what happened to him. Xenia, you said the colony here cleared the whole valley?"

"So they claimed, in any event," Xenia said.

"It certainly isn't clear now," Karl said. "So, the mantids got back in somehow."

"That's what we're here to find out," Quedra said. "Do you know where the main base was?"

"At the north end," Xenia said. "They built a station above the green zone, on the side of the mountain, and expanded down from there."

"Got it," Aoife said, peering through binoculars. "Looks pretty intact, but no lights."

"That's our first stop, then," Quedra said. "Zham, take us there. We'll drop down close and go in with the descender." She looked around at the crew. "The rest of you stay ready if the mantids get excited. Niko, Lanzo, I want you on deck. Zham, you and Karl are going down with Ingeborg."

The big woman grunted and walked off. Xenia said, "I should go as well. The professor will want a prompt report."

"It could be dangerous," Zham said. "The base isn't high enough to keep the mantids out entirely."

She drew herself up. "I can handle myself in the field."

Quedra caught Zham's eye and gave a pained shrug. Zham swallowed a sigh and nodded grudgingly.

"Better suit up, then."

The descender was less cramped when it wasn't stuffed with fuel tanks, and there was enough room for Zham to pace as they approached the base. The others looked out the windows or rechecked their equipment. Ingeborg once again carried her light machine gun and a backpack full of ammunition, along with a machete and several sidearms. Zham had his 1.1 pistol, and Karl carried an 0.9 with a distinct lack of enthusiasm.

Xenia wasn't armed—weapons in the hand of someone who didn't know what they were doing were worse than useless—but Zham was surprised to see that she *did* have appropriate gear, which had presumably spent the trip folded into one of those trunks. Heavy brown trousers festooned with pockets, a leather vest over a tough linen shirt, and a broad-brimmed hunter-style cap, all so new that the creases were still knife-sharp. Her vest pocket was full of pencils, and she toyed with one as the ground grew nearer. She was such the picture of earnest nervousness that Zham couldn't stop sneaking looks out of the corner of his eye. Was she *acting*? If so, it was the finest performance he'd ever seen—

With a *thump*, the descender landed on the roof of the base. Ingeborg adjusted the lev tanks, giving them just enough weight to stay put while being ready to ascend at a moment's notice. She checked her weapon one more time, opened the main door, and motioned for everyone to follow. The roof outside reflected the usual Academic obsession with domes and circles, sloping gently down from the center until it met a ring of smaller domes, like a big bubble surrounded by a ring of little ones.

The highest point was occupied by an antenna tower, and Ingeborg led them in that direction. There was a hatch at the base, leading to a shaft with a ladder stretching down into darkness.

"What exactly are we looking for?" Karl said nervously.

"The logbooks," Xenia said. "They'll be in the central control room, on the top level. They should tell us what happened here."

Zham looked skeptical. "If it was a crisis, would they really have updated the logs?"

"Victor was a good Academic," Xenia said. "Recording data is a sacred trust, even at the worst of times."

"Stay close," Ingeborg ordered, "and try to keep the noise down."

She clicked on a flashlight clipped to her chest and swung into the shaft, her heavy backpack nearly scraping the opposite wall. Zham and the others followed to the first landing, where a door gave access to a narrow maintenance corridor. Painted signs led them out into the halls of the base proper.

It was certainly more comfortable than Theovan had been, or, for that matter, than the *Last Stop*. The floor was carpeted, the walls plastered and painted a tasteful dove-gray. Framed pencil sketches of distant cities hung at regular intervals. With all the lights off, it felt more like poking through an abandoned hotel than a military installation. Xenia shone her light around, then pointed.

"This way."

At first, it was so neat that the inhabitants of the station might have merely stepped out for a moment, but as they went on, jarring notes began to appear. A cart full of files had been upended, paper drifting across the floor. Dripping water from a broken pipe in the ceiling created a moldy bloom. A large stain, brown with age, the plaster beneath rotting away.

"Either that's blood or someone spilled a hell of a cup of coffee," Zham said.

"No bodies," Ingeborg said, glancing both directions at an intersection before continuing onward.

"Mantids wouldn't leave any, though," Karl said.

"If this place had been stormed by mantids, it ought to be a lot more wrecked," Zham said.

"Not necessarily," Ingeborg said. "Bugs can be surprisingly neat."

"There." Xenia pointed. "That's the control room."

A pair of sliding doors were stuck without electricity, forcing Zham and Karl to pry them apart with the engineer's crowbar. Once inside, flashlights flickered around a large space, with a central plotting table facing three big television monitors and several wheeled blackboards. Ranks of desks filled the back of the room, each with its own typewriter, chairs overturned and files scattered as if in a desperate ransack.

"No windows?" Zham said, playing his light along the ceiling.

"These would be connected to external cameras," Xenia said absently, indicating the heavy glass screens. She made a beeline for a larger desk at the hub of the room.

It was one thing to know that the Academies were richer and more advanced than the Empire, but the reality was still a shock. Zham had only seen televisions in shop windows with absurd price tags attached, and in Aur Marka, most offices would have to share a single typewriter. And everything here was at least a decade old. He wondered, idly, what Academic aeros were like and how the Anark designs compared.

"Got it," Xenia said, hauling open a drawer. She hoisted out several ring binders and dropped them on the desk, raising a cloud of dust that made her cough. "This is going to be a lot to go through."

"Skip to the end," Zham suggested.

"Take it back to the ship," Ingeborg said. "Longer we're here, better the chance something goes wrong."

"Give me a few minutes," Xenia said. "Just to make sure this is what we need."

She flipped the last binder open and started to read. Karl poked gingerly through the maps and diagrams on the main table. Zham exchanged a look with Ingeborg and kept one hand on his pistol, walking the edges of the room in a slow circle.

"This place is enormous," Karl said after a while. "The aboveground station is just the start. They dug into the mountain and found natural caves." He squinted. "If I'm reading this right, you could fit the *Last Stop* down there."

"Caves?" Ingeborg said, frowning. "Mantids love caves."

Everyone simultaneously looked at the floor. Down at the edge of hearing, Zham thought he heard a distant scraping.

"We should go," he said.

"Agreed," Ingeborg said, hefting her big gun. "Xenia, is that the right book?"

"Oh, yes," Xenia said absently. "I'm trying to figure out—"

"Figure it out back on the *Last Stop*," Zham said. "Grab it and let's get back to the descender."

And then, he told himself, *it's time for all the secrets to come out.*

Everyone else breathed a sigh of relief once they were away from the ground, but Zham's tension only grew. He kept glancing at Xenia, who was still engrossed in the binders, flipping pages back and forth and ignoring the descender's gentle swaying. When they were back aboard, Zham had to prod the Academic to get her to look up. Once she stepped out, Zham grabbed Niko and dragged her aside.

"Stay with Xenia," he whispered. "Make *certain* she doesn't go to her room or use a radio. I'll go and get the"—he looked over his shoulder—"the thing, and we'll show Quedra and decide what to do."

Niko nodded nervously and hurried off beside the Academic. Zham went to Xenia's room, no longer bothered about who saw him, and gingerly lifted the leather-bound trunk onto his shoulder. He'd intended to talk to Quedra privately, but by the time he got there, she'd already gathered the entire crew in the mess hall to hear what Xenia had to say. Zham set the trunk down and stood in the doorway to listen.

Xenia was sitting cross-legged on a table, the three big binders open in front of her. Quedra sat in her wheelchair, impatience written on her face.

"Do you have everything you need?" she snapped, after a painful silent minute.

"I think so . . ." Xenia said, then shook her head and seemed to rise out of some sort of Academic trance. "Yes. Victor was indeed a good Academic. The story is here, all but the very end."

"So, what happened?" Aoife said.

"I should really inform the professor first," Xenia said uncertainly, looking to the door. Zham, blocking it, gave an insincere smile.

"I think we deserve to hear what we came all this way to find," Quedra said.

Xenia blinked, then shrugged. "I can't see the harm, I suppose. You know that Victor discovered this place and funded an expedition to claim it. Apparently, he met with great success, at least at first. He blanketed the valley with clingfire bombs to eliminate the mantids before landing soldiers and workers."

She seemed not to notice a slight shiver running through her audience. Clingfire was a legend for the Imperials, a distillation of mantid extract into an unstoppable incendiary that belonged to the Academies alone. They guarded the secret of its creation closely, and it had been a major factor in maintaining their independence.

"As expected, once they were burned out, there was no easy way for the mantids to return," Xenia went on. "Victor's people constructed the station, discovered the caves beneath it, and expanded it into a larger complex with entrances down in the valley. They built farms on the cleared land and even began the work of cleaning the algae from the lake. Victor covertly exchanged the produce of his farms for more equipment and other supplies, doing his best to keep the exact location a secret. But, as you know, at least one visitor left the description we followed."

"So, what happened?" Lanzo said. "It certainly isn't cleared anymore."

"About ten years ago, fresh mantid attacks began," Xenia said. "At first, Victor and the other leaders thought they were scouts coming over the mountains, and were content to hunt them down. By the time they realized the numbers were too great for that, farming had been seriously disrupted." She looked down and flipped a page. "They formed a perimeter, but it was too wide to defend with their limited manpower. Victor authorized bombing, in spite of the damage it would to do what they'd built, but only after things were too far gone.

"Too late, they discovered the problem. The mantids weren't coming over the mountains. There is another cave complex, at the other end of the valley where the lake drains underground to the plains beyond. The mantids found their way through it, first a few and then in great numbers. Victor sent an expedition to try and destroy the entrance, but they never returned. At that point, they'd been pushed back to the base itself and mantid fliers were in the valley. Their aeros and other vehicles were gradually destroyed."

In spite of everything, Zham felt a wince of sympathy. It was an old story, maybe as old as humanity. Mantids were huge and terrifying, but humans working together could defeat them with technology, whether that meant bows and spears or machine guns. But the bugs were *relentless*, pushing on with endless patience and brute indifference to losses. With their absurdly fast breeding rate, any battle of attrition was one the humans would inevitably lose, unless they retreated back above the green zone where the mantids couldn't survive.

"Victor says that he waited far too long before admitting the end had come," Xenia said. "He was down to a skeleton force defending the station." She frowned, tracing the words with one finger. "They were cut off from the lower levels, from someone named Leonid—another leader, maybe? But they had a small ship docked where we are now. Victor loaded his remaining people and tried to escape. On the last page he says that the ship is damaged and there are fliers everywhere."

"And, since news of this never got out, presumably they didn't make it," Quedra said.

Xenia looked up, and to Zham's surprise, there were glittering tears in her eyes, though her voice was steady. "The fact that he left these logs behind suggests that he did not expect to."

There was a pregnant silence.

"But," Aoife said, "he discovered the problem. The caves. If the valley were cleared again and the caves blocked off . . ."

"Then the whole project might work," Lanzo said. "Which means this is possibly the most valuable vacant real estate in the world."

"Unless there are more caves," Karl said gloomily. "Or Victor was wrong."

"Steady on," Quedra said. "I'm sure that's of great interest to the professor, but we're just finishing a job. Xenia, what else do you need to do here?"

"I'm not certain," she said. "These records need more study. My first step is to contact the professor and report. He may have further instructions for me—"

Zham took a deep breath.

"I'm afraid," he interrupted, "we can't allow that."

Another silence. Everyone in the room revolved to look at him, as though on turntables. Xenia seemed to be speechless, so it fell to Quedra, turning her chair in a slow circle, to ask the obvious question.

"What are you *talking* about?"

"I need to show you all something." Zham hauled the trunk through the doorway. "This is a piece of Xenia's luggage. I found it in her room—"

"What were you doing in my room?" Xenia said.

Zham waved a hand, hoping to elide that point. "—I *found* it and brought it here because I wanted everyone to see it. This belongs to you, then?"

"It looks like one of mine," Xenia said.

"Do you know what's in it?" Zham said, starting to imagine himself in a courtroom.

"I really couldn't say," Xenia grated, voice icy. "The professor's people packed a lot of my gear. Apart from my *personal* things, which I don't appreciate being poked through."

"That was my fault," Niko said. "I mean, ultimately, it's Xenia's fault for bringing it here, but—"

"*Please get on with it*," Quedra said, rubbing her temples. "What's in the damned box, Zham?"

"Do you have a key for it?" Zham said to Xenia.

Her brow furrowed. "None of my trunks are locked. I haven't got any keys."

She sounded so sincere that Zham hesitated a moment, but he quickly regained his aplomb. "Fortunately, we managed to open it regardless. And we found"—he flipped the lid back and stepped aside, like a magician revealing a trick—"this."

A third silence, of a very different character to the first two.

"Karl," Quedra said slowly. "What am I looking at?"

"That's a bomb," Karl said. He was standing very still. "Quite a large one."

"Exactly how large?" Aoife said conversationally.

"Large enough to destroy the *Last Stop*, if it went off in here," Karl said. "Or in Xenia's room. Or anywhere belowdecks."

"I've never seen that thing before," Xenia said. She had gone very pale.

"It's not armed," Zham said, "but I think we can all guess what the plan would be. Once we return from the mission, Xenia gets off, 'forgets' one of her trunks, and then—" He clapped his hands and everyone but Quedra jumped. "She and the professor make certain of our silence. Is that about right?"

Zham looked up at Xenia, who looked from him to the bomb and violently shook her head.

"Of course not!" Her accent thickened under stress, turning her *w*s into *v*s. "I would never participate in such a thing! And I cannot believe the professor would engage in such conduct, either. As an Academic in good standing, it would be shameful."

"Nevertheless," Quedra said, eyeing the trunk, "the bomb is here. It can only have come aboard with you."

"I— I—" Xenia sagged under her gaze.

"Also, it's armed," Karl said.

A fourth silence, of yet a different sort. Everyone looked at Zham.

"It's . . ." Zham looked down into the trunk, where a tangle of wires sat atop several large metal cylinders. "It can't be, right? There'd be a timer or something."

"Zham," Quedra grated, "*not all bombs have a big clock like in the kinema.*"

"It's not on a timer," Karl said, bending over the trunk. Sweat was starting to stand out on his face. "It's a radio detonator. A very long-range one—look, that whole coil is an antenna. When this gets the right signal on precisely the right frequency—"

Niko clapped, and this time, Zham jumped along with everyone else. Even Quedra looked a little perturbed.

"Frankly," Karl said, "I'm surprised it wasn't rigged to blow when the trunk was opened."

Zham hadn't thought about that. He felt sweat prickle his own forehead.

"Karl?" Quedra said. "Could you possibly do us all a favor and disarm the bomb before we discuss this further?"

Karl nodded. He pulled a work knife from its sheath and bent further, poking among the tangle of wires. The whole room held its breath as he found the one he wanted and wrapped it around the blade. The wire parted with a jerk, and fiery death failed to ensue. Everyone breathed out.

"So, she brought aboard a bomb with a radio detonator," Zham said, trying to recover his rhetorical balance. "That makes the plan easier, I guess—"

"They wouldn't need a long-range receiver if they were going to blow us up in port," Quedra snapped. "Think it through. Xenia got her luggage from the professor. The only reason the professor would have for destroying the *Last Stop* is to prevent the valley's location from leaking. As soon as we dock anywhere to let Xenia off, the secret is potentially blown. Therefore?"

Zham wasn't keeping up but Niko jumped in. "Therefore, he intended to destroy us out here! Hence the long-range receiver."

"But," Zham said, "Xenia would still be . . ."

He looked over at Xenia, who'd gone from pale to a rising crimson. She was staring at the trunk, muttering a string of profanity under her breath that would have done credit to a Lunachi fishwife. Her clenched fists shook with anger.

"Oh." Zham looked around at the faces of the others, then back to Quedra. "So, what do we do now?"

"I don't know yet." She continued rubbing her temples. "I need to think."

With impeccable timing, the alert klaxon gave out an ear-rending *blat*. At the same time, Elli skidded down the corridor, grabbed the edge of the doorway to stop herself, and gasped out,

"Martin says the *Move Fast & Break Things* just came down from the Layer! Six aeros already launched!"

CHAPTER NINE

A bare few minutes later, they reconvened on the bridge, minus Karl, who'd peeled off to the hangar deck to prep the aeros. Zham wheeled Quedra as fast as he dared up the purpose-built ramp, settling her in her usual place at the plotting table before grabbing a pair of binoculars and going to the window.

There was no disguising *Last Stop*'s terrible position. They were well below the Layer, which meant that the *Move Fast* had at least a kilometer of altitude on them. In a ship-to-ship engagement, being below an opponent would be a crippling disadvantage, even if *Last Stop* had anything to match *Move Fast*'s 10 cm guns, which of course it did not. *Last Stop*'s aeros would be in difficulty as well, with *Move Fast*'s circling fighters able to stoop on them at will.

One of the six aeros up there was a bright, bloody red from nose to tail. Zham didn't need to be told which of Gough's pilots sported *that* affectation.

"So," he muttered to Quedra as the others gawked out the windows, "what would the Diamond Knife advise about this particular tactical situation?"

"Something like 'Don't get yourself into it,'" Quedra said. "Not that we'd have a chance against them in a fair fight, mind you."

"What now, then?" Zham's eye was drawn to Xenia, who'd come in behind everyone else. Something in his guts flip-flopped, some emotion looking for a place to latch on, and he pressed it down hard.

"Hope Gough wants to negotiate," Quedra said.

As if on cue, there was a ping from the board. Martin glanced over and said, "Transmission from the *Move Fast*, ma'am."

Zham watched his sister's face harden. "Let's hear it."

"Hello, *Last Stop*," Gough said, his voice crackling from the speakers.

Martin set a microphone in front of Quedra, who said, "Hello, *Move Fast & Break Things*. Here for a friendly visit?"

"Can't say that I am," Gough said. "Not by my choice, though. I gave you people every opportunity. If Sa-Yool had taken Erich's advice back in Aur Lunach, none of us would be here."

Quedra clicked the mic off and raised an eyebrow in Zham's direction. He chuckled awkwardly.

"I guess I never got around to telling you that part. He tried to warn us off before we left. I didn't think it was worth addressing."

Quedra turned the mic back on and said, "We don't respond well to threats, Mr. Gough."

"Ms. Oserova could have come with me back at Theovan," Gough said.

"And when she wouldn't and we laid out your crew, you sabotaged our fuel tanks," Zham snapped.

"Only in the interests of peace," Gough said. "We figured on letting you stew a few days, then offering Ms. Oserova a more reliable ship to take her the rest of the way."

"So you could throw her over the side once you got here, is that it?" Zham said, real heat finding its way into his voice.

"Of course not," Gough said, but the grin in his tone was obvious. "We'd have found some use for her back in Newer Liberty."

Xenia spat another string of curses. Gough laughed.

"What now?" Quedra said. "I assume your interest in Ms. Oserova is ended."

"Regrettably," Gough said. "We're here, after all, and that makes you and yours inconveniently party to a very valuable secret. I'm afraid I won't be able to sleep at night until all of you and that arthritic rust-bucket are a smear on the valley floor. I just wanted to let you know that this is your fault. You backed me into a corner, and backing Harry Gough into a corner is *always* a bad idea. Erich?"

The Imperial nobleman's cultured voice broke into the circuit. "Yes, sir?"

"Over to you."

Sudden silence. Outside the window the *Move Fast* began to shift position.

"So, we're fucked, right?" Niko said conversationally. "That's the situation?"

"I am sure Quedra has something up her sleeve," Aoife said, but Zham could hear the uncertainty in her voice. "She's gotten us out of worse."

Zham watched his sister. Just for a moment he saw the mask slip, saw the terror and despair behind her eyes. There was no plan, there was *never* a plan, there was just improvisation after desperate improvisation until one day the last-minute long chance didn't pan out. And then people died. The meticulous, confident genius of Gor-Bel-Sul had perished at Gartop along with thousands of the Protectorate's best, when the Diamond Knife had shattered and her plans had fallen to pieces.

He'd wondered, from time to time, why Quedra had accepted her exile so meekly. Now at last he thought he understood. In her mind, she deserved it.

All that in a split second, the scary mental connection of two siblings who'd spent decades in close company. Then the mask was back up, Quedra's inner world hidden even from Zham, and of *course* there was a plan. There always was.

"We have to save what we can," she said. "We'll bring the *Last Stop* down close to the station and see if we can mask the descender, get everyone inside. If the Anarks don't know we're there and Lev and Karl can fix the radio, we might be able to contact someone for help once they leave."

That this was a slim chance was immediately apparent. Taking everyone into a station possibly full of mantids with no supplies and hoping to hide for an undetermined length of time could never be anything but. But Zham felt a swelling pride in the crew when, in this moment of crisis, nobody argued. Ingeborg, a silent presence on the back wall, gave a grunt of assent and turned away at once to start preparing. Zham looked at Aoife, Lanzo, and Niko, and found a determination that mirrored his own.

"We'll need time," Zham said. "If Erich's fighters start strafing us and spot the descender, the game's up. I'll hold them off as long as I can." He raised his eyebrows. "Anybody coming with?"

"*Obviously*," Niko said. "Wouldn't miss it."

"I'll take a bomb up," Aoife said. "If I can plant it on the *Move Fast*, maybe I can ruin Gough's day."

"And I'll be right beside you, my dear," Lanzo said.

The glance she shot him was mostly affectionate, which made Zham reflect that things must be *really* bad.

"Thank you," Quedra said. "We don't have time for a speech. Just go and try not to die."

"So, just to check," Niko said in Zham's ear, "this is a doomed-last-stand sort of thing, right?"

Karl, ahead on the flight deck, gave an "okay" sign and ran out of the way. "Better out here than in there," Zham muttered, after making sure the others wouldn't hear.

"Oh, absolutely. Just, you know, preparing myself. Girding my soul for the hereafter. You trust in any gods in particular?"

"Not really," Zham said. He'd burned incense when custom dictated, but he'd never put much thought into it.

"Me neither," Niko said. Her voice fell a little. "Maybe if I did, I wouldn't be halfway to pissing myself."

Zham gritted his teeth and punched back to the squadron frequency. "We can do this," he said. "Everyone knows Anarks can't fly, even if their kit is top-notch."

"Erich's an Imperial," Niko pointed out.

"I'll handle Erich," Zham said. "We take out him and his aeros, then ditch over the station. Float down and meet up with everyone. Once the Anarks leave, we call for pickup, head back to Aur Lunach, and see how chipper Gough is when he finds out he just declared war on the Empire."

"Oh, is that all?" Aoife said.

"Nooooo problem," Niko drawled.

"Barely one and a half of them for each of us," Lanzo said. "Hardly fair."

"You're set," Quedra's voice broke in. "Go at your discretion."

Zham glanced to make sure Karl was clear. Instead of the engineer, however, he saw Xenia looking at him from the shadow of the control tower. Her expression was hard to fathom, and his own emotional response felt equally confused, with vestiges of anger at her, anger on her behalf, and a solid helping of guilt, even though *he* could hardly have known—

Once again he crammed it down. Under the circumstances, it hardly seemed to matter.

Tell Zham that I wish he'd asked me out sometime.

Fuck. He almost cracked open the canopy to get out. But the others were on the deck behind him and there was no *time*. He stabbed viciously at the autoignition instead, and the DeFerra's big engine growled like it was hungry. RPMs climbed as he fed it bugblood. The aero started forward, faster and faster; he'd started from halfway up the deck to leave room for the others, so he shot off the far end before liftoff and went into a gentle dive, picking up speed as he went.

Behind him, Niko's springy little S-1 soared past, faster in a climb, and then Lanzo's Mercurio. Aoife came last in the Krager, the fighter-bomber taking the longest dip below *Last Stop*'s deck before climbing to meet the others.

"We're clear, Quedra," Zham said. "Get out of here."

"Fast as we can," Quedra said. "Just bail out somewhere we can catch you."

Overhead, the *Move Fast* was coming, descending slightly as it traversed the length of the valley toward the station. Zham wasn't sure exactly what the range on her guns would be at that altitude, but they couldn't have longer than a few minutes. Of more immediate concern were the six Anark fighters circling in two flights ahead of the cruiser. Rather than charging to the attack, they'd stayed at high altitude, waiting for *Last Stop*'s aeros to make their move.

Which was good, as far as it went. Less chance they'd see the descender when Quedra and the others made their escape. But it left Zahm with a tricky problem if he wanted to get at them.

"They're going to dive on us as soon as we start up," he said over the squadron link. "No way to prevent them from getting that shot, so let's make it their only one. Stay close on me and we go straight down their throats. Break on my signal—Niko with me, Lanzo stick to Aoife. Clear?"

"Got it!" Niko sang out.

"With you," Aoife said.

"Perfect," drawled Lanzo. "Let's go hunting."

Zham devoutly hoped they'd get that far. He opened the throttle as far as it would go and went into a steep climb, watching his rear-view and backing off a fraction when Aoife's Krager threatened to stall out. His 111's nose was pointed almost directly at the circling specks. They had the diffuse glow of the Layer behind them. It made them harder to see, but it wasn't like the Anarks were trying to hide . . .

"Here they come!" Lanzo said.

The specks shifted, growing rapidly. The Anark fighters had blocky, angular cockpits, squared-off wingtips, and green-striped wings. Zham looked for a bright red aero, didn't see it, didn't have time to worry. They were getting close, the familiar feeling of slow drift suddenly becoming shocking speed, and Zham waited until *almost* the time he'd have taken his own shot—

"Break break break!" he shouted, wrenching the 111 into a violent turn.

Blue-green tracer fire ripped past, stitching a line under his belly. By turning a moment too soon, Zham had ruined both their head-on shots, hoping to get into a maneuver fight. The Anark flashed past, already pulling out of his dive, moving too fast to track. Zham kept up his brutal turn, g-forces shoving his insides back and down, trying to get on the Anark's tail. He caught sight of the S-1 in the mirror, Niko staying with him—he couldn't see the others—

"More of them!" Aoife said.

Zham snapped out of his turn, instinctively rolling the other way before another shaft of blue-green tracer shot past. *This* opponent was bright red, like a burning brand slashing at the sky, with two more fighters on his heels. For a moment, Zham felt grudging admiration—Erich had held half his aeros back, knowing they'd be lost in the glow from the Layer and waiting until *Last Stop*'s fliers gave him easier targets. Good tactics, and now all semblance of formation had fallen apart.

The sky was full of twisting, shooting aeros, hard to distinguish except by tracer color. Zham looked for Niko and spotted Aoife instead, heading for the *Move Fast* and rolling side to side to avoid an Anark closing in from behind. The enemy pilot was too intent on their prey, letting Zham come up into their blind spot. Something tipped the Anark off the instant before Zham squeezed the button, though, and the lances of red fire aimed for the base of the engine instead walked backward along the body of the aero, leaving a line of holes and a trail of black smoke. The damaged aero peeled away.

"Thanks," Aoife called back. "Let me lay this egg and I'll return the favor."

Another Anark zipped by below. Zham rolled to dive in pursuit and spotted Niko in a rolling dogfight with another fighter, the two aeros looping after one another round and round, losing altitude with each pass. Her S-1 turned better than the heavier, more powerful Anark, and with one more circle, she got far enough over to fire a short, precise burst that stitched the other aero's engine with red tracers. It blazed up instantly, a roaring mass of flame, and the fighter peeled away in a desperate dive. Over the radio, Niko gave a wild war-whoop.

"Nice shooting!" Zham said. His own prey had outdistanced him, and he turned in Niko's direction. "I'm on your wing; take the lead—"

Another aero shot past, forcing Niko to take wild evasive action. Zham shifted to get onto the interloper's tail, only to realize it was Lanzo's Mercurio. He'd deliberately startled her aside and now turned back into a climb.

"Get clear!" Lanzo shouted. "They're coming down again—"

With a roar like a wild beast, Erich's bloodred fighter slashed down, two more Anarks flying on his wings. Lanzo, caught flat-footed, was a sitting duck. Erich's guns spat fire, the muzzle flashes blazing through his propeller, not machine guns but heavy 2 cm cannons. The explosive shells slammed into Lanzo's Mercurio, walking up one wing and across the cockpit, blowing the fuselage apart with multiple detonations until the whole aero went up in an orange-red fireball.

"*Fuck!*" Zham heard himself say as though from a great distance. Through the roaring in his ears he heard Aoife shouting over the radio, but his vision had collapsed into a narrow tunnel with a red aero at one end. He twisted into a dive, following Erich down, the 111 gaining speed with every moment.

The red fighter twisted, fast as a snake, and Zham followed into an upward spiral, first one way, then the other. There was no sense of panic in his enemy's movements, and even in his rage, Zham realized that Erich was testing him, pushing the limits of the 111 to see where his own aero had an advantage. Sure enough, after levelling out, the Imperial threw his Anark fighter into a turn tighter than Zham could follow, peeling away degree by degree. Furious, Zham stomped on the rudder and put the 111 into a skid, slipping sideways for a snapshot. He hammered the button and red tracers lashed out, but they fell well behind Erich's tail, and then the red aero was out of sight. Zham hauled the stick over, pulling the 111 out of a near-spin.

"Zham, *break*!"

Niko's voice. Zham's hand moved before his brain, banking the other way just in time for spitting blue-green tracers to zip past. He'd lost track of Erich's two wingmen, who'd circled away and come around for a pass at him. The first shot by without slowing, but the second was closing from above, curving into an inverted loop to stay on Zham's tail. Before they had a chance to level out, however, a burst of red tracers rattled across the rear of their aero, chopping the rudder and elevator to flinders. The Anark kept diving out of control, and Niko's S-1 zipped by, closing on the other enemy.

"Gods be *fucked*, you're good at this!" Zham barked, veering wildly.

"Thanks!" Niko yelled back. "I actually threw up on myself just now."

Something *boomed*, audible even over the roar of the engine and the chatter of gunfire. A trail of smoke traced a perfect parabola from the deck of the *Move Fast*, now high above, toward the *Last Stop* far below. Zham felt his heart lurch, but the shell went wide, exploding to starboard and just below the ship in an evil black cloud with a heart of orange flame. Another blast came from the Anark cruiser's after gun, this one bursting above and to port.

"Going in!" Aoife sang out. "Zham, be a dear and look after Niko."

"Wait—" Niko said, interrupted by the roar of gunfire over her radio.

The dogfight had scattered aeros all over the sky, and it took Zham a moment to even find the big Krager. He finally spotted it, nearly on a level with the *Move Fast* and closing rapidly from its port bow. The last Anark was settled on Aoife's tail, and only frantic jinking was keeping most of his fire from hitting home. As Zham watched, crisscrossing machine-gun trails snapped out from all across the *Move Fast*, trying to pinion the Krager in a spider's web of blue-green tracers. The fighter-bomber's left engine burst into flame.

Zham's throat was raw from shouting. "Aoife, *get out of there*!"

He had no idea if she heard. Black smoke billowed around the aero as the pursuing Anark sheared off rather than fly into his own anti-aircraft fire. Several streams of bullets poured into the Krager, but too late; it wasn't going to stop, an aero-turned–burning missile flying on momentum alone. It impacted beside *Move Fast's* sleek bow, blooming into the orange-red fireball of burning fuel; a moment later, there was a more substantial blast as Aoife's bomb went off, and a chunk of *Move Fast's* deck blew free and pirouetted into the air. Thick, oily smoke streamed from the gash in the cruiser. The ship pitched downward, shedding altitude.

Zham sincerely hoped Gough had been standing right at the point of impact. Whether he had or not, however, the Anarks weren't giving up. Both big guns kept firing, the blasts marching closer to *Last Stop*. Zham wanted to put the 111 into a sharp climb, to get close and see what havoc he could cause before they brought him down, but he spotted Niko cutting across his path in pursuit of an Anark. The enemy fighter was damaged, leaking smoke but still flying, and she was intent on finishing it off. Zham opened the throttle to join her, then saw a streak of red zipping down from above.

Now it was his turn to scream a warning. "Niko, break break break—"

He could admire the artistry, even as his throat closed and his stomach turned to bile. Erich's dive was precise because Niko was right where he wanted her, led across his gunsight by the Imperial's ailing wingman. He fired a short burst directly into the S-1's engine cowling. The little fighter's propeller burst apart in a spray of smoke, and it began trailing a licking tongue of flame.

"Bail!" Zham said, wrenching his stick around.

"I've still got control," Niko said, coughing as smoke filled her canopy. "I can—"

"Bail *now* before it blows! I'll come get you!"

He had no idea how that would be possible, of course. But Niko evidently took him at his word. The S-1's canopy flew open. Amid the trailing smoke, he saw a small body tumble over the side and plummet toward the ground below. Moments later, the S-1 blew apart in a shower of flames.

Zham brought the 111 around, circling lower. It was a dumb maneuver, too slow, leaving him a sitting duck. But Erich seemed content to wait above him, ready for a dive but not yet taking the shot. Beyond him, the *Last Stop* was trailing smoke from a hit to her stern. An explosion above the flight deck had chopped down the tower, sending the bridge and all of Quedra's maps and files spinning into space. Another shell landed amidships, penetrating deep before exploding, and the ship took on a sudden list as one of its lev tanks was punctured. Flames raged upward.

Zham couldn't see the descender. He couldn't see Niko. He closed his eyes.

"Fuck it," he muttered, yanking the canopy back and throwing himself over the side.

CHAPTER
TEN

Falling. It's almost peaceful, except for the knowledge that a sudden stop is waiting at the bottom.

There was a cord strapped to the back of his vest with a flat metal handle at the end. His fingers found it, then hesitated. The ground drifted closer. *Last Stop* was falling, slowly but surely, as fires devoured her. His faithful DeFerra-111 flew on in a shallow dive, heading for the side of the mountain. Below was a jungle full of mantids for whom he was nothing more than a convenient snack.

Samantha had chosen her pistol when they came for her. That had taken courage. All Zham had to do was nothing. He hadn't seen the descender make its escape; for all he knew, everyone aboard *Last Stop* was dead, his sister and Sev and Karl and the girls. Xenia. Lanzo was dead, Aoife was dead. Even Ingeborg might be dead, though in her case, it was hard to believe a mere flaming explosion could be fatal. And Niko—

Had jumped, because he'd told her to. She was down there somewhere.

He jerked the handle convulsively.

At the small of his back, tucked into his vest, was an expandable lev tank made from stiff rubber with a tiny bit of liquid lev in a pressurized capsule. The cord broke the capsule and ignited a magnesium strip, which instantly heated the now-gaseous lev to a roiling fury. In that agitated state, it provided enough levity to kill the momentum of his fall, with an overpressure valve letting it gradually escape so he could descend gently.

That was the theory, anyway. He'd been late triggering it, and the levity this close to the ground was consequently stronger. The force of its inflation was a ragged jerk, snapping his chin against his chest hard enough to leave him seeing stars. Time briefly became a flickering series of images—he saw the 111 ram the mountain in a spectacular bloom of fire, saw the trees reaching up to embrace him, and then blinked and found himself stuck in a crotch between two leafy branches, the deflated rubber bladder hanging down his back like some horribly prolapsed piece of intestine.

A bit of a rest, then, before moving. His chin hurt and his chest hurt, presumably at the spot where the two had come together. He waited for his head to stop spinning before risking a look around.

Fortunately, he was most of the way down the tree, and the ground was only a couple of meters below. He gripped a branch and lowered himself, realized he had farther to go than he thought, and tried to climb back up but didn't have the strength. Instead, his fingers slipped and he dropped, landing with a knee-shivering jolt on nearly bare earth. He'd bitten his tongue, and his mouth rapidly filled with a bloody tang.

Other than that, though, no harm done. Honestly, pretty good under the circumstances. Zham spat and unclipped his vest, letting the rubber bladder fall away. There was supposed to be a bail-out kit in the cockpit, but he hadn't checked it in years. In any event, he'd failed to grab it before jumping. That left him with the contents of his pockets and the 1.1 in his holster, with six bullets in the cylinder.

He'd landed on a sloping hillside, roofed over with jungle trees whose canopy spread high above and choked out the vegetation at ground level. Down there was a realm of semi-darkness, tree roots twisted all around like a writhing bucket of worms. Shelf mush-rooms clung to the trunks and other strange fungi poked up from the ground, capped with puffballs or inverted cones.

Ahead he could see daylight where a rocky stretch broke up the canopy. He began climbing to start in that direction, then froze. A dozen mantid fliers sat among the rocks, sunning their enormous wings in the glow from the Layer. They were considerably more intimidating from this vantage than when seen through the gun-sight of an aero.

Okay, Zham said to himself. *We need a plan.*

Step one, find Niko. He was close to the area where she'd ditched, but down there, that left a lot of ground to cover.

Step two, get inside the station.

Step three—well, he could worry about step three if he managed steps one and two.

He had a flashlight tucked into a pocket on his leg. The beam was clearly visible in the haze of spores and pollen under the trees. Zham shone it around, hoping Niko would see and know what it meant. He turned away from the fliers, moving deeper into the jun-gle, and cupped his hands around his mouth.

"Niko!" he said, in the half-shout-half-whisper of someone who both does and doesn't want to be heard. "Hey, Niko!"

Nothing moved. The jungle was silent as always but for the mutterings of distant gunfire. Zham clambered over a pile of roots as tall as he was, slid down the other side, and tried the flashlight again.

"Come on, Niko," he said. "Poke your head out before some-thing else does—"

Something shuffled in the tree above him. Zham spun around, hand dropping to his revolver, and felt a weight slap across his face and fill his mouth. He tried to shout but produced only a muffled squeaking.

"What the *fuck* are you doing?" Niko hissed, hanging upside-down by her legs from a branch. Her forearm was wrapped around Zham's head.

"Mmming fuh mmmoo," Zham managed.

"What?"

He pushed her arm away. "Looking for you," he whispered.

"You don't look by shouting," Niko said. She dropped, doing a neat flip and landing gracefully on her feet. "You're lucky it's me that found you."

"Yeah. Lucky." Zham looked her up and down. "You're . . . okay?"

"A bit singed," Niko said, brushing ash out of her hair. "Otherwise—"

He wrapped his arms around her, pulling her close with a surprised squeak. She wriggled for a moment, then relaxed into his fierce embrace, her head against his shoulder and her feet twenty centimeters off the ground.

"You're okay," he whispered.

"Yeah," Niko said softly.

A long moment passed.

"You smell like vomit," he said.

"I told you." She squirmed. "Can you put me down, please?"

Zham opened his eyes and a mantid was staring at him.

It was a warrior, emerald green and scythe-armed, huge compound eyes looking down in an almost quizzical fashion.

"Zham?" Niko said. "Down?"

"Mmm," Zham said, not moving.

"And yet I remain in the air," Niko said. "Curious."

"Mmmph," Zham said, hardly daring to breathe. The mantid was as still as a statue except for the twitching tips of its antennae.

"Which suggests," Niko said, "that one of them is right behind me, isn't it?"

"Mmmhmm."

"Wonderful." She let out a breath. "I'm open to suggestions."

Zham didn't have any ideas, but he didn't end up needing to admit it, because at that moment, there was an explosion. It was the deep bass rumble of something large blowing up a long way off, and it seemed to go on for some time. The foliage in the canopy rustled and a few leaves filtered down.

The mantid's head snapped round. It stood stock-still a few moments longer, antennae shifting, then bolted away from them. When it was out of sight, Zham gently lowered Niko to the ground, then leaned back against the tree trunk, breathing hard.

"That was . . . lucky," Niko said, looking a little pale herself. "What was that, do you think?"

"Had to be the *Last Stop* hitting the ground," Zham said. "A blast that size might draw every mantid in the valley."

"Buys us a little time, anyway," Niko said. She looked at him sidelong. "Did you see—before you jumped—"

Zham shook his head. "I didn't get a good look. But I've been assuming they made it to the station." Because if they hadn't, there was no point to any of this. "We need to get there too."

Niko pursed her lips. "That's going to be quite a climb."

"Maybe not," Zham said. "Karl said the complex went well down into the mountain and there were entrances from the valley floor. All we have to do is find one."

"Any idea how?"

He shrugged. "Move toward the station, I guess, and keep our eyes open."

Discovering in which direction the station lay was the next obstacle. Niko followed Zham back to the rocky slope, where the fliers had evidently taken to the air at the sound of the *Last Stop*'s destruction. From there, Zham was able to see the sky and orient himself on the surrounding mountains. The station itself was only barely visible, a collection of strange domes clinging to the rock halfway up the mountain face. There had *better* be an entrance down here, because Zham was certain he and Niko were never going to climb that high.

Even on reasonably flat ground, the roots and fungi made for slow going, as though the forest itself resented his intrusion. It was strange, Zham thought as he climbed, that what he thought of as normal—streets and houses and such—only held sway on a tiny handful of mountaintops, while most of the planet looked like this. Trees and mantids as far as the compound eye could see.

The silence ate at him until he couldn't take it anymore. Niko paused in the shadow of yet another vegetable barrier, hands on her knees as she gasped for breath. Zham leaned against the wood beside her.

"Up there," he said. "That was good flying. *Great* flying."

Niko made a face. "The part where my friends got killed, or the part where Erich shot me down?"

"You can't blame yourself for that. Everyone"—Zham's voice broke for a moment—"everyone knew what we were up against. Outnumbered by an enemy in superior aeros."

"I'm not saying it's my fault," Niko said bitterly. "But I'm not patting myself on the back about it, either."

"You did better than I did," Zham muttered.

Niko snorted as though it had been a joke, but Zham was sincere. As they started forward again, he found himself contemplating an uncomfortable truth—in the decade since they'd left the Protectorate, he'd lost his edge. He'd chided Quedra for her lack of ambition, but flying against mantids and half-trained pirates had made him lazy. And then, when it counted, he hadn't measured up. Niko had outflown him with an amazing talent and a rookie's verve, but that wasn't the worst of it. Erich's precise, careful, devastating maneuvers had once been the sort of thing Zham laughed at, the "flying by protractor" taught in the Navy's elite schools that he'd always spurned. But Erich had beaten him, neatly and comprehensively.

If I ever get another shot, Zham vowed to himself, *things are going to be different.* Then he nearly broke out laughing, because of course, wounded pride was the absolute least of his current problems, and getting into another duel with Erich seemed about as likely as taking on the whole Navy single-handed—

"Hey." Niko poked him in the ribs. "Am I crazy or is that a road?"

He broke from his reverie and followed her pointing finger. It took a few moments to spot the patch of asphalt, miraculously undisturbed by the surrounding roots. A few flecks of yellow paint still clung to it. Ahead, bits of broken-up road surface peppered the wood where they'd been lifted by the tree's writhing.

"I think you're right." The fast growth of the mantid jungle was legendary, but it still boggled the mind that all this had arisen in a mere decade. Zham imagined the ground undulating like it was full of snakes, saplings rapidly filling out into giants and shouldering aside the works of man. "Should we try to follow it?"

"Roads usually go somewhere," Niko said. "It's better than wandering aimlessly."

Having a direction lent Zham a bit more purpose, and he focused his attention on spotting more remnants of the old Academics. There weren't many—what the forest hadn't broken, the mantids had stripped. He spotted the engine block of a car, acid-pitted and held high in a net of branches. Tumbled stones, too square and regular to be natural. Broken-up bits of concrete and a steel bollard embedded in a trunk.

He froze when movement caught his eye. A ways off, mostly hidden by the trees, something was creeping along the ground. Zham caught Niko's shoulder, held a finger to his lips, and pointed. She nodded, and they continued their quiet progress.

There had been no more explosions, and the mantids had come down from their state of high alert. Twice Zham had to skirt clearings full of cows, one with multi-armed worker mantids tending to them. Scout beetles wandered about, their trundling gait oddly porcine, and when they came too close, Zham and Niko took cover behind a tree until they were past. Several times, Zham was certain they'd lost the road, but Niko always spotted another bit of asphalt further on. It led in the same general direction they'd been headed, into the mountains and toward the station.

They'd made it onto a rocky hillside when their luck finally ran out. Zham spotted a beetle behind them, and the ground was open enough that he was certain he'd been seen in return. Sure enough, while he and Niko dove for cover, the scout stood stock-still. Zham could almost see the puffs of pheromones drifting on the wind to summon its companions.

"The hill's getting steep," Zham whispered. "If this road goes somewhere, we must be close. Run for it?"

"What's the alternative?" Niko mouthed.

"Get eaten?"

"Running it is. On three. One—"

The beetle opened its wings and screeched. Niko took off like a startled rabbit, pelting up the remains of the road. Zham drew his revolver, sighted, and fired just as the thing sped forward—the first shot missed, but the second drilled it in the head, and it rolled over in a broken heap. The gunshots echoed through the forest, and suddenly, there was movement all around. Zham turned and ran, fear giving new strength to his aching legs.

Fear or not, he wasn't going to outdistance Niko. Fortunately, the farther he went, the more intact the road was, trees widely spaced as the hill got steeper. They seemed to be heading right for a sheer cliff, and Zham pulled up short at the sight of a door big enough for a truck set into the stone. Its two halves were firmly closed. Niko stood at the seam, prying at it with her hands.

"It's steel!" she shouted. "We're not getting through!"

"Is there a control box?" Zham said, turning to face the way they'd come. The skitter of many legs wasn't far behind.

"Over there, but there's no power!"

"Pull it open and see if there's a manual crank!"

Niko slapped the door one more time and sprinted for the box. Zham shifted to a two-handed grip, set his feet, and waited. A pair of scout beetles rounded the corner almost immediately, spreading their wing cases and making that horrific *scree*. Zham shot the first one before it could charge, missed the second by meters. He shifted his sweaty hands on the grip and nailed it as it closed.

"There's a crank!" Niko shouted.

"Well, crank it!"

"I'm cranking! Nothing's happening!"

Zham glanced over his shoulder. The doors *were* sliding apart but painfully slowly, the gap only centimeters wide.

"It's working! Keep going!"

Another beetle rounded the corner. Zham aimed, finger on the trigger, but didn't fire. One bullet left. Better wait until he couldn't miss—

A flash of green. A mantid warrior stepped out, four meters high, several more beetles scurrying around its spindly legs like a pack of hunting dogs.

Zham looked desperately over his shoulder again. The gap was still narrow—Niko might fit, but he never would. He stepped backward, gun still raised.

"Forget it!" he shouted. "Get through—"

"Go fuck yourself!" Niko yelled back, cranking furiously. "Almost there!"

The mantid stalked forward, antennae waving, beetles milling around it. Zham swallowed and lined up the sights. He offered a prayer to any gods that might be listening and squeezed the trigger. The 1.1 gave its vicious kick against his hand.

A stray god must have been listening, because it was the shot he needed, catching the mantid squarely in one of its compound eyes. The creature's head snapped back and its lower arms reached for its head in an oddly human gesture. One antenna hung limp and dead, while the other thrashed madly. All the beetles skittered wildly in a milling mass, spending a confused moment sorting out what had happened before turning back in Zham's direction. Their wing cases fluttered.

"Go *now* I'm not fucking kidding—" Zahm screeched, turning his back on them and sprinting for the door. Niko was ahead of him, reaching the gap and slipping through it easily, shoulder-first. Zham hit it a moment later, jamming his arm through and blowing out breath to flatten his stomach. The edge of the steel caught on his gunbelt, and he tore at the buckle until it came free, tossing the empty revolver away.

Too narrow. His hips were stuck, one leg through and the other dangling in the dirt like a fishing lure. He heard the beetles screeching, wings buzzing, but he couldn't even turn his head to watch them. *Just my luck*, Zham thought. *I'm going to die with my arse sticking out for a bunch of bugs to take a bite out of—*

The pressure miraculously loosened. Zham heaved, scraped forward another centimeter, felt it loosen further. He popped through, skin scraping free, and tumbled onto a metal floor.

"Get up get up get up!" Niko shouted. She was working furiously at another crank beside the big door. "Keep them out until I get it closed!"

Zham rolled over just as the first beetle hit the door. It was too wide for the gap, but it twisted itself to try to fit, mandibles snapping. A second one scrambled over the first, wedging itself in sideways. One of its wing cases cracked but it kept coming, working several legs through to the near side of the door.

Scrambling to his feet, Zham grabbed the flashlight from his belt and swung it like a club. Metal clanged on metal, and he heard a hoarse scream that he realized belatedly was his own. One beetle leg retreated and he bashed at the other until the joint broke. The lower beetle was solidly wedged, but its mandibles still clacked centimeters from Zham's stomach. He directed a kick at it, the sharpened chitin scraping his boot.

"Get out of the way!" Niko shouted.

Zham reeled back, flashlight at the ready. Niko's efforts steadily narrowed the gap, gears turning within the massive doors, and they came together with inevitable force. There was a *crunch* of chitin and a spurt of black fluid. Then they were closed, the seam still dripping. Zham slowly lowered his flashlight, butt end coated in oily black stuff.

"Holy shit." Niko leaned against the wall, holding her stomach. "Holy *shit*. We made it."

"We made it." Never mind to *where*. For now, the important thing was *away*. "You saved my ass."

"Obviously." Niko wiped her dripping forehead, spiky hair drooping with sweat. "You can thank me later."

"Remind me if I forget."

The only illumination came from Niko's flashlight, which lay on the floor. Zham switched his own on, mildly surprised to find it still worked after being used as a beetle-basher. Playing the beam around, he found they were in a tunnel, wide enough for two cars and several meters high. It curved away into the rock.

"This is really connected to the station?" Niko said, picking up her light. "It's still a long way above us."

"According to what Karl said when we were in there, yes." Zham found some numbers stenciled on the wall, barely faded. "Victor and his people did a lot of digging to expand the caves."

"But the mantids got in here in the end, right?" Niko said.

"Evidently." He glanced back at the massive door, which would have done credit to the warships he'd served on in the Navy. "Some areas might still be sealed off, though. Academics don't do things by halves."

"I guess we follow this, then," Niko said.

"And keep an eye out for a way up," Zham agreed.

"And hope we don't run into more bugs."

"That," Zham muttered, "probably goes without saying."

If not for the signposts on the wall at each intersection, they would have wandered forever in the dark like a couple of lost souls. Fortunately, the Academics had laid out the base with their usual thoroughness, and Zham followed the signs for the Main Hangar on the theory that a "main" anything was probably a good place to start. The big vehicle tunnel ended in a parking lot, several rugged six-wheeled cars still in their spots. Another sliding door on a more-human scale led deeper in. Without power, it wouldn't move, but Niko found a shovel strapped to the back of one of the cars and used it to crowbar her way in.

Zham kept the shovel with him for digging and/or bashing as they kept moving forward. They passed empty receptionist's desks and lines of abandoned offices full of typewriters, filing cabinets, and other paraphernalia. The aboveground station had indeed been only the tip of the iceberg; the operation here, Zham suspected, had been the size of a minor Navy base. This area was much neater than the levels above, everything carefully closed up and boxed away. Zham imagined workers being told their evacuation was temporary, early in the fight, before it became clear that all was lost.

There were signs there, too, on neat little boards, but their meaning was somewhat more cryptic. Acronyms and numbers labeled departments, corridors, or both. Zham kept moving toward the

"Main Hangar." Niko followed, staring excitedly at the fixtures revealed by their roving flashlight beams. For her, Zham imagined, offices were as foreign as the mantid forest.

Finally, they reached another sliding door with Hangar H-7 stenciled across it in foot-high letters. Zham pried it open with the shovel. As he pushed through the crack, he caught a familiar scent, the mélange of bugblood, oil, and metal that marked engines and heavy machinery. The echoes gave the sense of a huge space, and his flashlight revealed only more brushed-concrete floor, with no sign of walls or ceiling.

"This is something, anyway," Niko said. "Gods, look at the *size* of it. How are we supposed to find our way around?"

"Carefully," Zham said. He shone his beam back toward the door. "Maybe follow one of the walls?"

"There," Niko said, pointing out a bright red box with a heavy-duty knife switch. The sign beneath it read Emergency Power. "Think it still works?"

"Doubtful," Zham said.

Niko was already heading over. "I mean, if it works, we might get lights. If it doesn't work, no harm done, right?"

"Unless something explodes— Niko, wait—"

She threw the switch with a *clunk* and stepped back. Silence.

"I told you—" Zham began.

Something went *bang* in the middle distance, like a pistol shot. Zham spun, hand dropping to his holster before he realized it was gone. Then he recognized the familiar sound of an autoignition, followed by the sputter and cough of an engine coming up to speed. The rising whir was joined by several others. There was a sharp metallic *crunch* and squeal as something, somewhere had a bad day, but by then, his attention was elsewhere.

Overhead lights came on bank by bank with a series of *clunks*, like an army of illumination marching across the ceiling in hobnailed boots. The space they revealed was larger even than Zham had guessed, easily large enough to swallow the *Last Stop* or even the *Move Fast & Break Things*. That was good, since the main feature of the huge chamber was a ship bigger than either.

The surface they were standing on was part of a vast U shape stretching around both sides of the ship one level below the flight deck. The stern faced them, massive engine nozzles visible, and above the flat edge of the deck Zham could see the sleek, raked-back shape of the conning tower. Half-meter letters stenciled on the side named the ship the *Leonid*. The pit in the center of the U dropped down far enough to accommodate the vessel's boxy underside, with massive steel struts connected to broad pads that supported the ship's weight.

It was a drydock, in other words, a place for building or repairing a ship when her lev tanks were blown completely empty. The sides of the U were lined with huge tanks, cranes, hoses, and other equipment, all neatly stacked and stowed in anticipation of a return that had never come.

Niko gave an eloquent summary. "Holy *shit*! Is that a godsdamn fleet carrier?"

"Heavy cruiser," Zham corrected. "But yeah. Holy shit."

He'd never seen an Academic warship in person, though they'd been on the syllabus in training. While the Protectorate Navy had been eager to emphasize the minuscule size of its Academic equivalent, they hadn't been able to completely gloss over the fact that the Academies produced better engines, hulls, weapons, and so on, making use of military innovations that the Protectorate derided as unimportant and expensive affectations. A decade in exile had cured Zham of this snobbery, and the thought of getting to explore an advanced vessel for himself—not to mention whatever aeros were on board—had him practically salivating in spite of their rather desperate circumstances.

"Can it fly?" Niko said. "Tell me it can fly."

"You know as much as I do," Zham said. "But it stands to reason that if it could, they would have used it against the mantids, not left it down here."

"How does it get *out*?"

"There must be a hatch." Zham peered upward, but it was impossible to see beyond the blaze of lights. "I doubt it's going to be of much use to us, though."

"No, but that might," Niko said, pointing down the length of the ship.

A steel-and-wire tower ran up one wall of the big cavern and vanished beyond the lights. It took Zham a moment to recognize it as an elevator of the heavy industrial sort you might find at a mine. He gave it a skeptical glance.

"Everything down here has been sitting in the dark for ten years," he said. "You sure you want to trust your life to that?"

"More than I want to go back outside with the mantids," Niko said. She elbowed him in the ribs. "Come on; where's your sense of adventure?"

"I think I left it outside," Zham muttered. "With the mantids."

The elevator creaked, rattled, and groaned so much that Zham was seriously considering the mantid option by the time they reached the top. A set of substantial security doors opened on to a guard post with a desk. Loose papers were scattered across the floor, gathering dust. The décor looked similar to the part of the station Zham had visited, which he hoped was a good sign.

He quickly spotted another good sign behind the desk. A small cabinet contained a submachine gun of unfamiliar design, short-barreled and fed from a disc-shaped cylinder magazine. Zham grabbed it along with a couple of extras. There was an automatic pistol as well, which he passed to Niko. She looked at it without much enthusiasm.

"You know how to use that, right?" Zham said.

"Theoretically." She examined it skeptically. "I've never been what you might call a good shot."

"I'll take the lead, then." Not that it would *really* matter when the mantids found them. Still, the weight of the weapon in his hand made Zham feel a bit more confident.

The lights were on up there as well. Unlike the hangar, this place retained a decided feeling of panic from the evacuation, with over-turned furniture, abandoned bags, and the occasional old stain in the corridor. They came across a spot where someone had made a stand—a desk blocked the corridor, or had before it was broken in two. Bullet holes riddled the walls, and long stains in the carpet showed where bodies had been dragged away.

The main stairwell was easy enough to find. There was a simple map on the wall beside it, and Zham was relieved to confirm they were indeed in the station, on its lowest level. The control room he'd visited before was four floors directly overhead.

"This way, right?" Niko said, peering up the center of the spiral stair. "What are you waiting for?"

Zham tightened his hands on the gun's grip. He hadn't honestly expected to get this far, and now that they had, he couldn't help but consider the possibilities for what came next. If they reached the top of the base and there was no sign of the descender—or if there *was*, and there were no survivors—

Focus, he told himself. His breath came fast.

"I'm coming," he said. "It's been a long day."

"Tell me about it," Niko said, though she looked as bouncy as ever.

They climbed two flights, and Zham poked his head out of the stairwell for a cautious look. He led Niko toward the edge of the cylinder-shaped station, padding through empty corridors until they reached an outer wall. The rooms lining that side were all large, impressive offices with wide windows of thick, heavy glass. From there, Zham could see the valley stretching out below and the Layer glowing weakly up above. A huge column of thick, oily smoke issued from a patch of blackened jungle in the middle distance, which had to be where the *Last Stop* had found her final resting place.

To his surprise, he could see the *Move Fast & Break Things* as well. The Anark warship had lost most of its altitude, hanging above the valley a bit lower than the station itself. It was listing toward its front right quarter, which meant that Aoife's suicidal attack had probably damaged the lev tank there. That likely explained why they were so low as well—the remaining tanks would be straining to keep the ship aloft, and they'd function better at a lower altitude.

"At least we hurt the bastards," Niko muttered, pressing up to the glass beside him.

"It's something," Zham said. "But it means they're not going anywhere until they make repairs. If we're planning to wait them out, it may take a while."

"I don't have any pressing engagements," Niko said cheerfully. "And I bet there's food down in the hangar."

"Ten-year-old food."

"They've got to have some mantid jerky or something." She raised her eyebrows at his questioning look. "What, you've never had mantid jerky? It's good!"

"We didn't all grow up on a trawler," Zham said, pushing away from the window. "Okay. We head for the roof. If the descender reached the station, we ought to be able to see it from there."

The main stairwell ended at the top level, and they had to venture out again to look for the maintenance stair. Instead, they found trouble in the form of a troop of scout beetles hurrying through a crossing corridor. Zham was staring at the markings on the walls, looking for something familiar, and Niko had to yank him into a darkened office to hide.

"Mantids," she said breathlessly.

"Mantids," Zham agreed. "Which is probably a good thing."

"I don't think mantids are ever a good thing."

"The place was empty the last time," Zham said. "Something must have drawn them up here."

"Great," Niko said. "How do we get past them?"

"Hopefully, they're still distracted." Zham leaned out of the office; for the moment, the corridor was clear. "Come on."

They skulked forward. Twice more they spotted bugs and threw themselves into cover. A mantid warrior lumbered past, followed by a trio of skittering workers, smaller and without scythe-arms but still equipped with deadly mandibles. Zham held his breath until they were gone, suddenly aware of the sweat coming off his body and the smells it must carry to mantid antennae.

When he finally found the service shaft, they seemed to be nearing the center of mantid activity. The door was on the wrong side of yet another intersection, this one occupied by two scout beetles trundling around in a circle like a pair of dogs chasing one another's tails. Further on, several mantid workers were methodically chewing another door off its hinges, though the office beyond was empty as far as Zham could see. He and Niko took shelter in a bathroom, pristine aside from a layer of dust.

"They have to be here," Zham said. He checked the cylinder on the submachine gun, realized he'd just finished checking it, and jammed his hand in his pocket. "They have to be *right there*. What else are all these mantids doing?"

"The problem is they're right there and we're right *here*," Niko said. "And I don't see how we're supposed to change that."

"I thought you were the one with a sense of adventure."

"There's adventure, and there's sticking your head in the mantid's mandibles," Niko said. "Which, now that I think about it, is a distressingly literal figure of speech in this case."

"So what? You want to retreat?"

"Just for now," she said soothingly. "This is high altitude for the mantids. Eventually, they'll leave, right?"

"Sure, once they've eaten Quedra and the rest."

"If they haven't already." Niko's expression froze as soon as the words left her mouth, aware she'd made a mistake. "Sorry. Obviously, they haven't— Zham!"

He grabbed a couple of rolls of toilet paper on his way out the door. When he looked outside, the workers had gone, but the beetle guards were still in the intersection. Zham waited until their circling had them both facing away from him, then hurled a toilet paper roll so it sailed over their heads and bounced down an adjoining corridor. Both beetles turned in that direction, advancing cautiously toward this unexpected interloper.

"Zham, are you *crazy*?" Niko hissed.

"I'm going," Zham said. "If you want to go back, I'll meet you at the stairs."

He hurried out before she could answer. By the time he reached the intersection, he heard her quiet swearing close behind as she scuttled to catch up. The beetles were only meters away, prodding the roll with their mandibles; he could have rushed up and put his hands on the back of their chitinous wing cases. Zham's knuckles were tight around the trigger guard. They crossed the intersection in silence and kept moving toward the maintenance door.

"Okay," Niko said. "That was officially the stupidest thing I've ever done, and let me tell you, there's some *strong* competition—"

"Shhhh." Zham grabbed the door and took a deep breath. "Through here, up to the roof. Find the others, get them back to the hangar."

"Somehow." Niko shook her head. "Right. Let's do it."

Zham opened the door and looked right into the face of a mantid worker.

He'd never been so close to one before, alive or dead. There was more detail in its mouthparts then he'd realized, a whole set of interlocking jaws below the scissor-like mandibles, edged with roughened, knife-like strips of chitin for tearing flesh and grinding bone. The huge compound eyes reflected his astonished face a hundred times over, each facet showing him a different angle. He wondered if that was how mantids saw the world, a hundred slightly different versions of the same thing—

His finger jerked the trigger of the submachine gun without any conscious thought. The sound was shatteringly loud in the enclosed space, like rapid hammerblows to the ears. The gun bucked upward in his hands like an animal trying to escape. A line of 1.1 slugs walked up the mantid's spindly chest and shattered one of the compound eyes, leaving a ruin of sludgy black blood. The creature folded in on itself, legs thrashing spastically. Beyond it in the stairwell he could see several more.

Niko was saying something, but all Zham heard was a ringing like a hundred dinner bells. She grabbed the back of his shirt and pulled, pointing.

The two beetles from the intersection had turned around, following the noise. At the same time, several more worker mantids had piled into the far side of the corridor. One of the beetles opened its wing cases, the *scree* only barely audible in Zham's traumatized ears. He opened fire again, blowing both of them into twitching fragments, then took off at top speed, trusting Niko to follow.

The station closed in around him like a maze, its logical layout turned into a nightmare by a net of rapidly converging insects. A half dozen beetles blocked the direct route back to the stairs, so he turned into a side corridor only to find another worker coming around the other end. A burst felled it, the magazine clicking empty. Zham yanked it out and struggled to fit another one as he ran. Behind him, more mantids were closing; Niko turned periodically to shoot over her shoulder, putting holes in the carpet, walls, and ceiling but not hitting any actual mantids, even by accident.

"I *told* you I was a terrible shot!" she screamed, barely audible. Zham didn't have the breath to answer.

Around another corner. A beetle screeched and charged. Zham shot it, then spun to hose down the crowd that had come after them. Another magazine emptied. He rammed the last one in, tearing his finger open trying to work the slide. Niko covered him, *bam bam bam*, putting a neat constellation of holes in an office wall on all sides of a startled worker.

"Run!" Zham roared, bringing the gun up. He shot one more pursuing worker, then turned down another corridor. His fuzzy mental map indicated this ought to be the way back to the main stairs, but the route didn't look familiar—

"Zham, *Zham*!" Niko yanked his sleeve, pointing around the next corner.

It was a dead end, the hallway letting on to a bank of conference rooms rather than cutting through like he'd imagined. Zham spun, finding the corridor behind him crammed with mantids. The sub-machine gun roared, spitting fire until the magazine gave out and it emitted only a muted clicking. He let the weapon fall to the floor with a clatter, smoke curling up from the barrel.

Niko solemnly handed over her pistol. Zham took it without a word, checked the magazine, and dropped into a firing stance. The end of the hallway was awash in broken bugs and black blood. It was hard to tell what, if anything, remained intact. For a moment, there was no movement, and Zham had the foolish hope that he'd somehow wiped them out—maybe it had only been a scouting party—

A warrior stepped around the corner. It was hunched forward, antennae scraping the ceiling, scythe-arms held at the level of his head.

"Oooookay," Niko said. She grabbed his shirt at the small of his back, her hand twisting the fabric very tight. "We're dead. We're dead we're dead we're dead." Her voice had gone very small. "Please shoot me I don't want to be eaten please please please . . ."

Zham shot the mantid instead. He aimed for the head, hoping for a repeat of his feat outside the door, but that kind of luck didn't strike twice. The pistol didn't have the stopping power of his 1.1, in any case. Sparks flew as bullets ricocheted off the warrior's carapace or smashed the plaster of the wall. When the gun was empty, the creature began stalking forward.

He wondered if he ought to have saved one for Niko or for himself. *Tell Zham that I wish he'd asked me out sometime . . .*

A deep-throated roar like a metal lion, and the mantid staggered sideways. Bits of it blew apart as its carapace cracked. A lucky shot caught its stick-thin neck and sent the head spinning away across the corridor. The body fell into a heap of gore, and the hammering sound stopped, replaced with footsteps. Ingeborg came around the corner, machine gun still braced against her hip. She looked at Zham and Niko, gave a nod as though they were exactly what she'd expected to see, and offered them an approving grunt. Behind her a small, grubby face peeked around the corner.

"It's them!" Elli shouted. "I said it would be, *actually.*"

Zham tossed his gun aside, fell to his knees, and sobbed in desperate relief.

CHAPTER
ELEVEN

Everyone who'd been left on the *Last Stop* was crowded into the elevator. Ingeborg, methodically changing the barrel on her machine gun. Martin, imperturbable as ever, with a rifle on his back. Karl, carrying Anni on one shoulder; the girl's arm was bound in a makeshift sling, and Zham could see the pain on her brave face whenever the elevator lurched. Elli hovered nearby, only a little too old to wrap herself around her father's leg but clearly wanting to. When Niko knelt beside her, however, the girl happily flung her arms around her neck.

To Zham's astonishment, Aoife was among the survivors, her right leg heavily bandaged. She leaned on Quedra's cane for support. When he first saw her, Zham's eyes practically popped out of his head, and he quietly confirmed that this apparition was visible to everyone else as well. Then he hugged her until she rapped him on the head and told him to loosen his grip.

"I bailed out, didn't I?" she said, when questioned on her survival. "I wasn't going to stick around for that. Got a little souvenir courtesy of some Anark gunner, but by the time my tank inflated, they had bigger things to worry about and I had plenty of sky to steer over to the station." She shrugged. "Bit woozy by the time I got down, though."

Sev, goggles on, pressed their diminutive form into a corner and muttered to themself, uncomfortable outside of *Last Stop*'s warren-like engine deck. Zham made a mental note to check in with them in private; of the crew, they were certainly going to take the loss of the ship the hardest.

And, of course, there were Xenia and Quedra. The former was carrying the latter on her back, arms around her neck and legs at her hips. Quedra managed to make it look dignified, as if she were carried off doomed ships all the time. Xenia, on the other hand, looked more disheveled than Zham had ever seen her, her jacket missing a sleeve, her tie gone and hair escaping from its braid. Her eyes had lit up at the sight of him, but since then, she'd retreated back into her shell, playing the role of Quedra's loyal but silent mount.

"If anything," Aoife said, "*we're* the ones who should be surprised to see *you*. When I got down, they told me you and Niko had bailed out into the forest."

"It's a long story," Zham said. He glanced at Niko, and she shrugged. "Well. Not that long. We dodged mantids, got inside the station, and came to find you." At that moment, the elevator came out of the rock and started descending the last few stories to the hangar floor. Zham pointed. "We found *that*, too."

Karl gave a low whistle. Sev pressed up against the grating, goggles fixed on the Academic ship.

"Ain't that the damnedest thing," they muttered. "You know what that is?"

"A heavy cruiser," Zham said. "Right?"

"An *Academic* heavy cruiser," they said. "Damn me, she's pretty."

"The question," Quedra said quietly, "is what in the hells she's doing here."

"And how intact she is," Karl said.

Further speculation was momentarily curtailed by the arrival of the elevator at floor level. There was a pause while the crew ransacked the dockside supplies, which ended up producing enough fabric for a couple of makeshift hammocks plus crates to push together for a table and chairs. Karl—the closest thing they had to a doctor, though his medical training only amounted to an emergency first-aid course—changed the bandage on Aoife's leg, which was gory all down to her ankle, and rewrapped the sling on Anni's arm. She and her sister clambered into one hammock and Aoife took the other, closing her eyes and announcing that she intended to sleep for quite some time. The rest of the crew gathered around the table, where Xenia had already settled Quedra.

"All right," Quedra said. "We're all alive—"

"Except Lanzo," Zham said.

There was a pause as everyone looked down for a moment.

"Except Lanzo," Quedra said. "Who there'll be time to mourn when we're certain the rest of us will stay this way. Zham, are we secure in here?"

"I think so," Zham said. "We didn't see any evidence mantids had broken in. The outer doors are a half-meter thick, and so are the ones at the top of the elevator shaft."

"It's a wonder the Academics didn't hole up in here," Niko said.

"Prob'ly worried about getting trapped," Sev said gruffly. "That ship ain't ready to fly."

"And they had another docked up above," Xenia said. "Victor ordered an evacuation. He must have thought some chance of escape better than none."

"How long will the electricity last?"

"There are six generators," Karl said. "One of them's pretty badly busted, but the others look solid. Maybe a week's worth of bugblood in them. There's also these." He indicated the big tanks beside the docks. "I haven't had the chance to check them, but some of them have to be fuel. We can carry it over in jugs if we need to."

"I found food!" Niko said excitedly. "Dry rations and cans. There's stacks and stacks, and barrels full of water."

"It seems like they were getting ready to provision the cruiser,"

Quedra said. "Since that's a crew of a hundred or so and there's only eleven of us, it ought to last for a while."

"So, we can survive," Xenia said. Her agitation strengthened her accent. "But what are we going to *do*?"

"Sev, any chance of getting the cruiser off the ground?"

"Eventually? Sure. Soon?" They shook their head slowly. "Engines were still under construction, and now it's sat here for ten years. I can probably bodge something and get it limping, but we're talkin' weeks at best."

"Which brings us to our biggest problem," Quedra said grimly. "Gough and his crew are still out there, and they can't let us live, not if they want to keep their secret. Right now, he doesn't know we're here, but if we try to call for help or do anything obvious, there's nothing to stop him coming down here and finishing us off."

"Except the mantids," Niko said.

"That's not exactly a comfort," Zham muttered.

"I thought we were going to wait for him to leave," Karl said.

"The *Move Fast* is damaged," Zham said. "He'll have to make repairs first, and by then I bet he'll have backup on the way. Once they get here, we'll have no chance."

"Agreed," Quedra said. "We need to either get past him or take him out before that happens."

"Take him out?" Karl scoffed. "With what, harsh invective?"

"What about the aeros on the cruiser?" Niko said. "There should be some, right?"

Sev shrugged. "Prob'ly. Flight deck and hangar look complete."

"They'll be in bad shape after ten years," Karl said. "Canned food ages a lot better than aero engines."

"What are the odds you could get one flying?" Quedra said. "Use the others for spare parts?"

The engineer pursed his lips and gave a reluctant nod. "Likely. I'd have to see what we're working with, of course."

"One aero," Quedra said. She looked at Zham and Niko. "And two pilots."

"Against an Anark cruiser?" Karl shook his head. "Might be kinder just to wait for them down here."

"I'll fly it," Zham said immediately. "Whatever you need."

"Of course you will," Quedra said softly. "All right. If you all could . . . leave me alone for a while. I need to think."

The little group broke up, Karl to tend the injured, the two engineers to examine the cruiser, and the rest simply *away*. Zham hesitated, then took a few steps after Xenia. Before he could catch up to her, however, Quedra's voice called him back.

"Not you, Zham. Stay here."

He turned. The only other person left was Martin, and Quedra waved him away in spite of his obvious concern.

"I need to talk to my brother," she said. "See if you can find a bed or make up another hammock so I can rest when we're done."

"Of course, ma'am."

"Sit," Quedra said to Zham, patting the table.

With mounting concern, Zham took the seat next to her. Quedra hunched over the table and stretched her ever-rebellious legs, allowing pain to show on her face.

"Are you all right?" Zham said quietly.

"No." Quedra closed her eyes. "I'm tired."

She leaned toward him, not quite touching. Zham froze like a kid on his first date, unwilling to move in either direction.

"It's been a long day," he managed.

"It's been a long decade," she said. "All I wanted was a . . . a job. A decent life for both of us. But this is all I know how to do, and flying is what *you* know how to do. I thought . . ." She trailed off.

"That's not what you told me when we left the Protectorate," Zham said. "We were going to build our own fleet. Show everyone."

"I thought you needed . . . something like that." She swallowed. "All I wanted was to be ordinary again."

"You were never going to be ordinary," Zham said. "I knew that when I was fifteen. I knew it when I followed you to the Empire."

"You shouldn't have done that," she said quietly. "Uncle would have taken care of you."

He put on a half-smile. "But look at all the fun I would have missed out on."

Quedra laughed, too high and too quickly. She leaned a fraction farther, her head resting ever so gently against Zham's shoulder, as though she were ready to yank it back in case of rejection. Zham glanced over and was astonished to see tears in her eyes. He couldn't remember the last time he'd seen her cry, not since they were children.

Very slowly, he raised his arm and fitted it around her shoulders. His sister turned her face to him, blotting her tears on his stained jacket, and spoke in a low whisper.

"I'm tired, Zham. My leg *fucking* hurts and I don't know what to do. I think we're all going to die here."

"You'll come up with something," Zham said, and immediately regretted it. He remembered the glimpse he'd gotten aboard *Last Stop*, the moment of panic. He felt her tense beside him. "*We'll* come up with something. You're the Diamond Knife and I'm Zham Sa-Yool, aero pilot extraordinaire."

"I didn't *want* to be the Diamond Knife," she said. "Not after Gartop. The Diamond Knife was a lie. But when I tried to be ordinary, to be *safe*, it all fell apart."

Zham thought back over the last few years. Quedra pulling herself in, making herself small. Taking the quiet road, the safe route. He'd thought she'd lost her edge, but she'd dulled it deliberately, trying to be something other than the leader she instinctively was.

No wonder she wasn't happy. He felt sympathetic pain deep in his chest and tried to breathe.

"I think," he said, "that you need the Diamond Knife more than anyone."

"She's not going to help us this time," Quedra said. "I deal in plans and probabilities. What we need now is a miracle."

"Let's make a deal, then," Zham said. "If I can deliver a miracle, will you think about trying to start over? Like we planned, but for real? I believe you can do it, even if you don't."

Quedra sat up, red-eyed, her features composed again. She wiped away tears and smoothed her hair.

"If you can get us out of this," she said, "I suppose I'm prepared to believe anything."

It was several hours before they reconvened. Outside, the sun would be slipping toward the horizon, the glow of the Layer reddening with twilight. In the hangar, there was nothing but the harsh overhead lights and the steady chug of the generators.

"I have a plan," Zham said to the group. He looked over his shoulder at Sev and Karl. "We think it'll work."

"Let's not go that far," Sev said.

"I said you'll get off the ground," Karl muttered. "*Probably*. After that, I make no guarantees."

"*I* think it'll work," Zham said. "But if it doesn't, it's going to put everyone here in danger. Gough will know we're here. We might be better off staying quiet, hoping he never finds us or that we can surrender to his people when they get here." He looked to Quedra. "It's your decision."

"Only if everyone agrees," she said. "The *Last Stop* is gone. I'm not a captain of anything anymore." She let out a breath. "But for what it's worth, I think we should try it."

"I support you, of course," said Martin.

"Obviously," Niko said.

"I took a bite out of Gough," Aoife said. "Only fair that you get to finish the job."

Ingeborg, occupied cleaning her machine gun, gave a distracted grunt that was probably an affirmative.

Sev let out a sigh. "S'pose it's the better of two bad options."

Karl glanced over at the hammock, where the twins were sleeping in a tangle of limbs. "I . . ." He rubbed at his face. "Fuck. I just want to get them out of here. Zham, promise me you won't fuck this up."

"If I do, you can get an apology from the flaming pieces of my corpse," Zham said.

Karl smiled slightly through his fingers. "Very reassuring."

Zham turned to the last silent figure at the table. Xenia startled slightly. "Do I get a vote? I'm not part of the crew."

"There is no crew anymore," Quedra said. "Just people trying to stay alive."

"Then I say yes," Xenia said. "Take the chance. I want to get back to Aur Lunach and spit in the professor's eye."

Zham closed his eyes, relief mixing with the realization that he would actually have to do it. "I'll need a tail gunner, then." He looked around the table, trying not to focus on Niko. She jumped up anyway.

"Planning on replacing me?" she said, in mock offense.

"I just didn't want to volunteer anybody," Zham said.

"Hmph." Her grin was back. "After all the years we've been together."

"Weeks."

"Same thing."

"So, what, actually, is the plan?" Karl said. "Apart from horribly dangerous and so on."

Zham glanced at Quedra, and she gave him a stiff nod. He took a deep breath and told them.

Silence.

Then Aoife, shoulders shaking, broke into wild laughter. She wiped at her streaming eyes with her hands.

"Sorry," she said. "Sorry. I shouldn't laugh." She shook her head, still grinning. "You guys are *definitely* going to die, though."

In some ways, getting out of the underground hangar was going to be the hardest part.

They'd found ten aeros neatly stowed on the cruiser's hangar deck. Karl and Sev had spent a frantic hour going over the best of them, replacing tubing, seals, and other parts time had ruined. According to Karl, they'd gotten lucky, but it still took three tries before the big twin engines turned over and raised a steady growl.

The elevator to the flight deck didn't work since the ship had no power, so that meant rigging a cable from one of the backup generators. Sev's almost-magical ability to know the functions of unfamiliar parts at a glance was all that let them get the job done before dark, but it was still approaching sunset by the time everything was ready.

And then there was the final variable: the surface hatch. This was a pair of mighty doors concealed under a layer of soil, big enough to allow the cruiser to lift off. In theory, they'd been built to last, like the rest of the Academic installation. In practice, Zham wasn't sure if even their careful engineering could cope with the rampant growth of the forest up above. But there was only one way to find out, and doing so would start the clock—Gough would easily see the doors opening from the air.

Zham sat in the unfamiliar cockpit of the Academic aero, parked at the very back of the cruiser's flight deck, and went over the controls one more time. There was nothing fundamentally different from the Krager or his poor lost 111, and certain conventions—stick, rudder pedals, throttle—were universal, but every nation seemed to have a different way of laying out instruments and other controls. He kept losing track of which was the altimeter and which the tachometer.

"You looking good back there?" he said.

"Feeling a little lonely," Niko said, her voice crackling over the shaky intercom. Unlike the Krager, where the rear gunner sat directly behind the pilot, the Academic aero had a separate rear canopy. "How's the weather up there?"

"A bit overcast," Zham said, glancing up at the big doors. "But I'm hoping it'll clear up. You're sure you know how to bail out?"

"Yes, *Mom*," Niko said. "By the way, I've got a bogey at three o'clock."

Zham looked to the right and saw Xenia coming across the flight deck. He pulled off his helmet and popped the canopy while she mounted the folding step to the cockpit. She'd shed her jacket entirely, her white shirt creased and gray with sweat, tie long gone. Her hair, released from its braid, hung past her shoulders. She kept one careful hand on her spectacles. When they came face to face, she hesitated, and Zham sought for something to say.

"Hi," he managed eventually, feeling like an idiot.

"Hi," she said automatically.

Another silence, except for the tinny encouragement yelled by Niko coming faintly through his headset.

The problem was that he had no idea where, exactly, they stood. There'd been . . . something, some kind of connection—unless it had been completely in his imagination, which, historically speaking, was pretty common—but that had been before he'd accused her of being a murderous traitor. She'd been exonerated, kind of, and it hadn't been his fault, kind of, but *since* then—had it really been just this morning?—there hadn't been time to clear the air. And now . . . what?

"What Aoife said," Xenia began. "That you're definitely going to die. Is it true?"

"You mean, is this a suicide mission?" Zham forced a grin. "I don't do those. We'll be back."

"Good," she said. "I mean, that would be good. I would . . . like that."

"Me too," Zham said like an idiot.

Another silence.

"Just kiss already!" came Niko's distant voice over the earpiece. Zham slapped at switches until it went quiet, not sure if Xenia had heard. He cleared his throat.

"You helped Quedra get away," Zham said. "I wanted to thank you for that."

"Somebody had to," Xenia said.

"Thank you, regardless." He took a deep breath. "If we do get back to Aur Lunach, after you spit in the professor's eye, would you like to go out to dinner with me? I know a great place on the third tier. It's not Talbot's, obviously, but . . ." Her expression had gone strange and he trailed off. "Sorry. Never mind—"

"Yes," she said. "After the eye-spitting, I would be happy to go to dinner with you."

"Great," Zham said. He felt, absurdly, like a weight had been lifted. "It's a date. I mean, it doesn't have to be a date, just sort of a figure of speech—"

"I think right now, you have somewhere to be." She slapped the edge of the cockpit. "But you wouldn't stand me up, would you?"

Zham grinned at her. "I wouldn't dare."

Xenia gave him a hesitant smile in return, then stepped back from the aero. Zham let the canopy close and put his headgear back on, flicking switches until he could hear Niko's heavy breathing.

"How could you not let me listen!" she said.

"If you wanted to listen, you shouldn't have been shouting advice."

"If you don't want advice, stop being such a total wimp!"

"How many dates have *you* been on, exactly?"

"I," Niko declared smugly, "just have high standards."

"Zham?" Quedra's voice sounded in his headphones. "Are you ready?"

"I think so," Zham said, cutting Niko off with a flicked switch. "Unless I've missed an explode-at-launch toggle somewhere."

"Lovely." The vulnerability from earlier was completely gone from her voice, replaced with stern authority. "Start your engine."

He hit the button. The autoignition went *bang* and both engines caught almost immediately, three-bladed props blurring into striped discs. The gauge that didn't move, Zham figured, had to be the altimeter.

"Looking good," he said. "Open it up."

"Gods have mercy," Quedra muttered.

Nothing happened for a moment, and Zham briefly wondered if the whole project would be reduced to a farce. Then, high above, something groaned, and there was the clatter and squeal of tons of metal shifting. A rain of soil began to patter down, carpeting the cruiser's deck in two slowly separating streams. He winced as a small tree tumbled down and caromed off the bow.

Overhead, a long line of reddish daylight spread into a widening rectangle, fuzzy at the edges with accumulated organic clutter. It reached half the width of the cruiser, then abruptly stopped with a screech of gears. Bits of root and broken branches swayed along the edges.

"I hope that's wide enough for you, because that's all we're going to get," Quedra said. "The trees up there must have tangled it. Sev says any more and we'll blow the motors."

"It's wide enough," Zham said, eyeballing the gap with the certainty of long practice. In any case, it wasn't the width he was worried about; it was the length. The hangar doors were designed for the cruiser to rise more or less straight up; while they gave the ship plenty of leeway, it was going to be tight for an aero to climb out.

"We're really going to make that?" Niko said.

"I think so." He'd measured it using the navigation tools on the cruiser's bridge, and Quedra had checked his math. But he couldn't know, exactly, how the Academic aero would perform. "Ready to find out?"

"If I said no, would you let me down?"

Zham grinned and shoved the throttle forward. He still had the brakes on, letting the engine ramp up as high as it would go. This would be the opposite of taking off from a ship above the Layer with kilometers of sky beneath you. No room for second chances. He tweaked the propeller pitch, flipped the fuel mix as rich as it would go, anything to give them a little more power. The aero started to buck and shudder against its restraints.

"Here goes nothing."

He let the brakes go. The Academic fighter leapt forward, quicker than he'd expected and gathering speed with each passing second. The engine roar rose to a howl and gauges spun toward the red. Zham ignored them, eyes glued to the end of the deck, silently counting.

Four . . . three . . . two . . .

On the *Last Stop*, they'd have fallen over the bow by now; thank gods the cruiser was bigger—

One—

He hauled on the control stick. The aero's nose tipped up, wheels clearing the ground with a meter to spare. Any other takeoff and that would mean they'd made it, but he kept pulling back, turning the ascent into a steep climb, seeking the narrow patch of red-gray cloud visible through the door. The far end of the hangar now seemed horrifyingly close. Over his headphones he heard Niko scream, half in excitement and half in terror. G-forces pulled him tight against his seat.

Climb too fast and you stall, as every novice pilot was taught. Stall there, in this concrete box, and die. Climb too slow and hit the hangar wall without reaching the surface. In between, the narrowest of windows, or maybe no window at all.

You could *feel* the stall coming if you'd done it a thousand times before. The wings shook, the whole aero shuddered, but you could tell if it had a tiny bit more to give. Just a little bit more—or else you were fooling yourself, you'd lost your edge and you were about to die—

The lip of the door passed below them. Zham swore he heard a *screech* as stray roots scraped across their belly, the unforgiving metal centimeters away. Up ahead were trees, tilted at crazy angles where the opening doors had partially toppled them. He jerked the stick violently, curving to avoid branches that seemed like reaching claws. The aero shot through, a storm of leaves swirling in its wake, and he finally levelled out just meters above the treetops.

"Holy *fucking* mantid *cocks*," Niko said. "Holy shit. I was sure we . . . Oh, *gods* . . ." She let out a long sigh. "Even if sex is all it's cracked up to be, it *cannot* be better than that."

"It's less likely to end in a fireball and twisted metal," Zham said, feeling distinctly postcoital himself. He reflected on his own experience for a moment. "Somewhat less likely, anyway."

"We can go home now, right?"

"Nah." Zham pulled into a thankfully gentler climb. "That was the easy part."

Half the sky was dark, the sun dropping rapidly toward the horizon and leaving behind a Layer flaming a dim red. Against that backdrop it was easy to spot the *Move Fast & Break Things*, a dark shape hanging above the jagged outline of the mountains. Somewhere up there, alarms would be sounding—while they might have missed a single aero, there was no way they hadn't noticed the enormous pit opening in the forest.

That pit was already closing beneath them to keep the mantids from getting in. Zham tried to look down as he circled over, but there were too many moving shadows to spot any bugs. If a few slipped through, at least Ingeborg was there with her machine gun to sort them out.

His own worries were more airborne. *Move Fast* would be launching any aeros it had on standby, and he kept looking for a familiar streak of crimson. It was too much to hope that Erich wouldn't come after him, but at least he wouldn't have much backup—several of the Anark aeros had gone down in flames and a couple of others had been damaged. With the cruiser itself in need of repair, Zham guessed the fighters were a low priority.

"Fliers coming up," Niko said.

"How many?"

"Just a couple, looks like. And they're headed for the door. Four o'clock."

Zham turned in a lazy arc and spotted the pair of mantids, their long, heavy bodies outlined against the glow of the clouds. They were flying straight and slow, the relaxed pace of a casual investigation rather than the fury of a swarm. The hive had noticed the shifting of the forest floor but wasn't yet on full alert.

"Time to wake them up," Zham said.

He slid into position for a diagonal pass, easy as firing at a target sleeve. The gunsight on the Academic aero was an unfamiliar design, but the markings were easy enough to figure out. He waited until the range was short and hit the button for a quick burst. The aero had six machine guns, all in the wings, and they chattered in an off-kilter drumroll. Brilliant green lines of tracers slid across the mantid for a split second before winking out.

As he'd hoped, the hits weren't enough to kill the bug outright. Its wings were wrecked, but it was still writhing as it went down and, more importantly, trailing a spreading, invisible cloud of pheromones. The second flier reacted instantly, slewing to a hovering stop in a way no aero could have managed, mandibles clacking as it scanned the sky. They were well past, but it charged in pursuit regardless, spreading its chemical message to its brethren all the while.

"Shrieker time?" Niko said.

"Not yet," Zham said. "Let's agitate them a bit more. Get ready to fire."

He recognized the rocky shelf near the spot where he'd first landed. At the time, it had been occupied by resting fliers, and by the red glow of the setting sun he saw that it still was, though they were starting to move and flap their wings in agitation. Zham came at them in a shallow dive, overcoming his own instincts to conserve ammo and firing a too-long burst that stitched through the little clearing from one end to the other, cutting one bug nearly in half. The others practically leapt into the air, and Niko opened up on them enthusiastically, the green line of her bullets sweeping into the gathering night.

"Should I be trying *not* to hit them?" she shouted over the machine gun's clatter.

"Plenty more where they came from!" Zham shouted back.

Then a glint of red glow from above made him slam the stick over, maneuvering violently and spoiling Niko's aim. Another aero roared past, dive now well off the mark, coming back into a climb to turn his speed into altitude again. Zham didn't need to see the color to know who was at the controls. A light blinked on his radio, and he flipped a switch.

"Zham Sa-Yool, I presume," came Erich's cultured voice. "You really are full of surprises."

"Only when I need to be," Zham said, turning back the other way as Erich maneuvered for another pass. "I'm really quite boring when nobody's trying to kill me."

"Under other circumstances, I'd quite like to hear where you found another aero," the Imperial said. "However, I'm afraid my employer is quite insistent that I destroy you with all haste."

"Yeah, but have you considered," Niko put in, "that your employer's an asshole?"

Erich dove again. Zham faked complacency, then jinked just as the red fighter came into range. At the same time, Niko opened fire, green tracer crossing blue-green as she tried to track Erich through his dive. His cannon shells detonated when they hit the ground below, throwing flickering, eerie shadows.

"A sell-stick cannot demand good behavior from those he works for," Erich said, as calm as if he hadn't just tried to blast them to bits. "Only that they pay on time."

Zham clicked the radio off and spoke to Niko. "Any chance you can hit him?"

"Doubt it," she said cheerfully. "Not while he's diving like that, anyway."

"He's not dumb enough to come in straight and level," Zham said. "And we're not going to outmaneuver him in a two-seater."

"So, what now?"

"We get this done. Start the shrieker."

Instead of the purpose-built device they'd had on the Krager, this was something Karl had bodged together in the last few minutes before launch. The sound it made was a hideous warble that rose and fell, and Zham had to hope that it pissed the mantids off just as much. He climbed, slowing abruptly and throwing off Erich's pursuit for a moment, but the red fighter simply circled for another try. Once again, Zham had to admire the Imperial's cool tenacity—many opponents would have been tempted to get in close and tangle, but the Academic fighter's tail gun made that chancy. Erich knew his advantage lay in fast diving passes; no matter how Zham swerved, his luck would run out eventually, and his heavier aero had little chance of turning the tables. He wondered if Erich could hear the sound of the shrieker and guess what they were planning.

Mantid fliers were appearing across the valley, drawn by the explosions, noise, and the diffusing chemical alarm. They rose from the trees, assembling into slowly growing swarms that circled like flocks of buzzing ravens, looking for the source of the problems. Zham aimed straight for the biggest group he could see, already dozens strong. He heeled the aero over as he came close, sheering off. The whole pack swerved in his direction, drawn after the sound of the shrieker like iron filings chasing a magnet.

"We've got 'em!" Niko crowed. "Gods, that's a lot."

"Let's collect some more," Zham said.

He watched Erich in the mirror. As the red aero tipped over, Zham threw his own into a hard turn. He'd used that trick once too often, however, and Erich was wise—he rolled, delaying the start of his dive, then came down once Zham had committed to the turn.

"About to get bumpy!" was all he had time to shout, wrenching the stick back the other way. The Academic aero responded beautifully, g-force pulling his stomach down into his guts, but it wasn't enough to shake Erich completely. Blue-green tracers stabbed out, and Zham heard the heart-stopping *ponk ponk ponk* of bullets striking metal. Erich zipped past, pulling into a climb.

"Niko!" Zham wrenched the aero back to level, rapidly running his eyes across the instruments. "Hey, talk to me. You okay?"

"Somehow," she sang back. "There's a few more holes back here than there used to be."

"As long as they're not in *you*." Erich's cannon must have missed the mark, and they'd taken only a few stray machine-gun rounds. Too close. "Hang on."

The deadly dance with the mantids was just getting started. He had to stay close enough to keep their attention while staying out of their reach. This time, there was nothing to defend, so he had a bit more leeway, but the slower speed he had to maintain left him even more vulnerable to Erich's passes. On the other hand, the increasingly crowded sky brought its own problems for his opponent. The light was steadily leaking away, and the mass of mantids grew shadowed. Plowing into one would be a bad way to die.

The groups of fliers had started to merge into a single swarm, whipped on by alarm pheromones. The cloud of them lurched in Zham's direction, amoeba-like, pseudopods made of hundreds of fliers reaching out to snare him. There were more than he'd expected, so many they were blotting out what was left of the sun. Behind and above him, he saw Erich lining up again.

"Time to get out of these skies," he said. "Start shooting when I signal and don't stop."

"Aye, aye!"

He dove, heading for the treetops just before Erich started his pass, the added speed taking him directly under the mass of mantids. The red fighter sheered off, unwilling to risk passing through the swarm. One worry removed. The remaining problem, however, was the mantids themselves. They dove straight after him in increasing numbers, plummeting past like falling bombs.

"Now!" he shouted.

Niko opened up, tracer fire stitching into the bottom of the mantid cloud, blowing apart several pursuing fliers as they tried to close. All the groups had merged now into one spectacular swarm, every flying mantid in the valley united in the single purpose of destroying the aero and halting the terrible sound. Acid spit sprayed all around, light drops spattering the windscreen and raising hissing trails of smoke from the wings. Zham pushed the throttle up and dove lower, trusting to speed, watching the cloud of descending mantids for a glimpse of the far side. If he didn't get past before he ran out of altitude—

"Come on come on come on—"

There. Clear sky past the buzzing horde. The aero shot out from beneath the swarm, bullet-fast, and Zham immediately went into a sharp ascending spiral, climbing as rapidly as his engines would carry him. The mantids followed, whipped and goaded by Niko's bursts of gunfire, rising up in a great cloud like a boiling thunderhead.

"What in the name of all the gods are you doing?" Erich said over the radio. Zham could see the red fighter circling the ascending cloud of mantids, climbing too, trying to find a way in. Massed bugs stretched up and up and up. "Have you gone mad?"

"*Kill him!*" Gough's shout over Erich's radio was so loud it was faintly audible to Zham. "He's bringing them up *here*, kill him *now*, you worthless mantid-fucker, what the *fuck* do I pay you for, now now *now*—"

Zham rose, circle after circle. The mantids were getting closer, bursts of spittle rising nearly level with the aero before falling away. Ahead of him, above him, loomed the darkened shape of the *Move Fast & Break Things*, engines suddenly flaring to life. All at once, a dozen anti-aircraft turrets opened up, machine-gun tracers criss-crossing the sky ahead. They converged on him, slashing into the mass of mantids, the broken bodies of fliers tumbling from the sky. Zham felt impacts from both directions, bullets stitching across his wing and streaks of acid drawing smoke from his tail.

"What a *show!*" Niko was laughing, high and hysterical.

One more second. The *Move Fast* grew larger still. One more second, and it filled the windscreen. One more second. The right engine burst into flames. He stopped circling, tilting the aero up and up until it stalled, wings shuddering wildly. His throat was hoarse when he shouted into his headset.

"*Kill the screamer!*"

He jammed the stick forward. Saw the screamer fall away in the rearview—Niko had thrown the whole thing out the canopy window. Mantids streamed upward like an aerial river, free of the sound they despised but now focused on a new target, huge and noisy and spitting gunfire in all directions. He could *hear* their bodies hitting the *Move Fast*'s outer hull, dozens of crushed insects falling away or blown apart by gunfire, hundreds more taking hold and tearing through metal with jaws and acid.

The Academic aero fell, tipping forward from a climb into a nearly vertical dive. Mantids zipped past, too fast to see, so close he heard the buzzing of their wings. Part of the tail ripped away with a *thump* and the skin of the left wing flapped loose.

The air started to clear. Gently, so gently, Zham eased back on the stick. He felt like he was flying a machine made of toothpicks and chewing gum. Any sharp move would tear something loose, break something off, send them smashing into the forest floor. But the trees were getting bigger and bigger, the altimeter whirling downward. Gently—gently—gently—

Up above, there was a series of explosions. Bit by bit, the windscreen filled with sky instead of ground. The altimeter slowed, slowed, slowed, and finally settled.

They were flying. One engine trailing thick black smoke and the other starting to stutter, but still straight and level. Zham's knuckles ached where he'd gripped the stick like a lifeline.

"Are we alive?" Niko said.

"Don't jinx it," Zham said, trying to convince himself to start breathing.

The sun was entirely gone, the last of the light draining from the sky. Above them, another fireball cut through the gathering night, showing a dark shape surrounded by a thousand tiny dots like it was seen through a haze of static.

"We . . . might be alive."

"Yeah," Niko said, voice thick. "About that."

Something moved in the rearview. A sleek red aero, paint marred here and there by acid spit. It slid in directly behind them at a matching speed. Zham dared not maneuver for fear of disrupting the fragile alchemy holding the aero together. It would be the easiest of easy shots for Erich, and all he could do was hold his breath.

"An interesting gambit," Erich said over the radio. "And well played. My compliments, Sa-Yool."

Zham waited in silence.

"I think that we both have a difficult road ahead of us," Erich said at last. "I wish you good luck with it."

Then he banked away, climbing into the night.

"Wow," Niko said after a while. "Is he going to try and help Gough?"

"I doubt it." The red aero was headed north, away from both the *Move Fast* and the station. "I'd bet he's headed home."

"*Home?*" Niko said. "He can't have enough fuel for that, can he?"

"He's got a lev tank," Zham said. "He could get above the Layer, turn the aero into a levship, use the wind, only run the engine . . ." He trailed off and shook his head. "A good pilot might try it. A *really* good pilot."

Silently, grudgingly, he added, *Good luck to you, too.*

"Speaking of really good pilots," Niko said, "how exactly are we going to land?"

Zham laughed out loud. "Land? Straight down onto the cruiser? Are you crazy?"

"Soooooo . . ."

"Get ready." They were getting close to the station, and he was reasonably sure they were over the area where the hangar door opened. Zham set the controls to keep the aero level and yanked the canopy open. "Jump for it!"

This time, at least he was ready for the jerk of the emergency lev tank inflating. He saw Niko hanging in the sky beside him, illuminated by the yellow light of a locator beacon. Together they drifted down toward the invisible forest while, on the other side of the valley, the tumbling hulk of the *Move Fast & Break Things* became a glowing smear of fire across the side of the mountain.

EPILOGUE

Zham, used to the Protectorate Navy's aggressively spartan décor or the *Last Stop*'s shabby chaos, found the bridge of the Academic cruiser somewhat overdecorated for his liking. The captain's seat was a wingback armchair that belonged in a drawing room, not on a warship, and all the furniture was polished wood with brass fittings. He had to admit, however, that Quedra looked regal, settled on the wine-colored velvet. Sev had gotten the ship's facilities working, including the showers, and Quedra's skin was clean and her hair back in its immaculate ponytail. Everyone's wardrobes had gone down with the *Last Stop*, of course, so her clothes still showed the rigors of yesterday. They were still searching for the ship's laundry.

The walls of the bridge were huge windows of reinforced glass, with the captain's chair facing the view across the flight deck. Zham could see Niko playing football with the twins, while Aoife sat in a folding chair and shouted indiscriminate encouragement. Martin and Xenia were busy hauling cables and tubes across the deck, running them into the elevator shaft from the supply tanks on the dock. Deep below, Zham knew, Sev, Karl, and Ingeborg were working on the engines; the old engineer had sucked their teeth at the sight of them, which was probably not a good sign, but they'd set to work regardless.

"They're a good crew," Quedra murmured, echoing Zham's thought. One of his thoughts, anyway. Xenia had stripped to a sleeveless undershirt in the heat, and that was proving somewhat distracting. Quedra must have caught the direction of his gaze, because she added, "I told her she can stay, if she likes. Given that her last employer tried to kill her."

"She'll want to go home to the Academies," Zham said, a hollow feeling in his chest. Their first date, he'd realized, could well be a goodbye.

"You might be surprised," Quedra said. "I hope she stays. Gods know we could use an accountant; I'm hopeless at it."

Zham risked a look at her. "We're keeping the company going, then?"

"You don't approve?"

"Oh, I approve. I just wondered, after what you told me . . ."

"When the mighty Diamond Knife broke down sobbing on her little brother's shoulder, you mean?" Quedra said. She reached down and straightened her legs, rubbing idly at knots in her thigh. "I was . . . not in a good state. You don't have to worry about any of that."

"Quedra . . ." Zham turned away from the view and stepped closer to her chair. "You don't have to shut me out again. You can trust me. Let me help."

She met his eyes and, after a moment, gave a crooked smile. "I suppose I should, shouldn't I? Given that you saved all our lives twice over and so on. It'll mean more work, though. You're sure you wouldn't rather just leave it all to big sister and disappear back into drink and debauchery when we get back to civilization?"

"I think I've had enough of debauchery," Zham said. At Quedra's raised eyebrow, he added, "For a while, anyway. So, what's the plan?"

"About what you'd expect," she said. "Get this ship in the air, limp back to Aur Lunach, and find someone to take it off our hands. It needs a serious refit, but it ought to be worth enough that we can buy something more in our class. Then pick up where we left off and try to be a little more discerning in our choice of clients."

"The ship's not the only thing we could sell," Zham said. "We have the location of the valley, too."

"Good luck selling *that* without getting killed in the process," Quedra said. "Xenia's professor knows, too, and maybe Gough's backers. It won't stay secret for long, which is all the better for us. Once it's out there, there's no reason to try and shut us up."

Zham gave a slow nod. He looked around the well-appointed bridge, out at the dock, the station above it. The valley, so well placed, girdled by its protective mountains like a miniature version of the Cradle.

"Or," he said, "we could keep it."

Quedra's eyes narrowed. "Keep what? The ship? We can't—"

"Keep all of it. The ship. The station. The valley. Gough and the professor both wanted to claim it for themselves. Why shouldn't we?"

"There aren't nearly enough of us, for starters."

"We'll recruit," Zham said promptly. "I know plenty of people in a dozen cities who'd jump at the chance."

"That all costs *money*. We'd need supplies, material."

"Borrow. Use the ship as collateral. The valley itself."

"No one is going to lend us money on land we don't even own!"

"Investors, then. Start a joint-stock corporation, offer shares. Find backers." He grinned at her. "I know a certain prince who owes you a favor. He'd be glad to hear from you."

"Don't remind me," Quedra growled. Her eyes searched his face. "You're serious."

"Sure. It's not enough to just *survive*." *Not*, Zham silently added, *for you*. "We can *build* something. Maybe it's a pipe dream to stick it to the blockheads back in the Navy, but at least we can have something to show them."

Quedra cocked her head. Behind those glittering eyes, he could see wheels turning that had remained still for a long time.

"It would never work," she said eventually, "to just claim the valley ourselves. It's not about the money or the people. The Imperial cities won't just stand by and let some upstart mercenaries set up their own domain."

Zham sighed, deflating. She was right, of course. It had been a nice thought, but—

"But if we were to find a *patron* and offer vassalage," Quedra went on, "then *that* would be a different matter. We'd have someone on the political side who'd defend our interests, because they'd line up with ours."

"And a patron would have to be powerful," Zham said, his smile slowly returning. "Which means rich. So, they could also be our primary investor."

"We'd be taking on certain obligations," Quedra said. "If our patron went to war, we'd have to assist."

"Good advertising," Zham said, waving a hand. "We'll need to get the word out. Clear the mantids from the valley, bring in colonists. We can learn from Victor's mistakes."

"If we could get this ship fully repaired . . ." Quedra said. "There aren't many sell-stick heavy cruisers, and those there are have long-term contracts. We'd have our pick of clients."

"Especially with Fleet Admiral Quedra Sa-Yool at the helm," Zham said. "Famed victor of Gor-Bel-Sul and all that."

Quedra hesitated, but only for a moment. She leaned back in the chair.

"It would be a lot of work," she said. "A lot of risk. And it could easily all be for nothing."

"Probably," Zham said. His smile widened. "It would take a miracle."

Quedra stared into space, one finger tapping against her teeth. The rust had fallen from the wheels now, and they were spinning full speed.

"That's another thing I wanted to ask you," he said. "Have you thought about the name of the ship?"

She blinked. "Hasn't it got one?"

"Some dead Academic." Zham shrugged. "Doesn't mean much to us."

"Did you have a suggestion?"

"I thought, perhaps . . ." He cleared his throat. "The *Diamond Knife*?"

Very slowly, Quedra began to grin, wide and wolfish, a predator staring at an unguarded flock. It had been a long time, Zham thought, since he'd seen that smile.

"That," she said, "sounds perfect."

Django Wexler is the author of flintlock fantasy series the Shadow Campaigns, epic fantasy series Burningblade & Silvereye, YA fantasy trilogy the Wells of Sorcery, and middle-grade fantasy series the Forbidden Library. In his former life as a software engineer, he worked on AI research and programming languages. Wexler currently lives near Seattle with his wife, daughter, four cats, and a teetering mountain of books. When not writing, he wrangles computers, paints tiny soldiers, and plays games of all sorts.

DISCOVER
STORIES UNBOUND

PodiumAudio.com